Raven Winter

ALSO BY SUSANNA BAILEY

Snow Foal
Otters' Moon

Praise for *Snow Foal*

'I absolutely love *Snow Foal* – it's so truthful, tender and touching. A book to read in a day and remember for a lifetime.' Dame Jacqueline Wilson, author of the Tracy Beaker books

'How much my daughter and I enjoyed *Snow Foal*! It's a gripping, sensitively written book.' Jenny McLachlan, author of *The Land of Roar*

'A mesmerising new voice about a girl that deserves to be heard.' Joanna Nadin

'One of my most highly-anticipated reads of the year.' Hana Tooke, author of *The Unadoptables*

'A tender, lyrical tale for a cold winter's night that will lift the spirits and warm the heart.' Steve Voake

Praise for *Otters' Moon*

'A beautiful story, immersed in the wild and restorative power of nature. I loved it.' Gill Lewis, author of *Sky Hawk*

'Sue writes with sensitivity and understanding about two children struggling to navigate complex emotions and situations.' Julia Green

'An excellent book – haunting and lovely. A delightful work of art.' Anthony McGowan

Raven Winter

SUSANNA BAILEY

For Gabriel and 'Apple', who never got to fly free

First published in Great Britain in 2022
by Farshore, an imprint of HarperCollins*Publishers*
1 London Bridge Street, London SE1 9GF

farshore.co.uk

HarperCollins*Publishers*
1st Floor, Watermarque Building, Ringsend Road Dublin 4, Ireland

Text copyright © 2022 Susanna Bailey

The moral rights of the author have been asserted
A CIP catalogue record of this title is available from the British Library

ISBN 978 1 4052 9996 1

Printed and bound in the UK using 100% renewable electricity at
CPI Group (UK) Ltd

1

Typeset by Avon DataSet Ltd, Alcester, Warwickshire

Chapter head and text break birds © Shutterstock

MIX
Paper from
responsible sources
FSC™ C007454

This book is produced from independently certified FSC™ paper
to ensure responsible forest management.

For more information visit: www.harpercollins.co.uk/green

ONE

The cold woke Billie: icy fingers poking through the cracked windowpane above her bed, crawling in her hair. So much for Daniel *getting that window sorted* last week. A bit of parcel tape, that was all she was worth to him. And that was already loose and flapping in the breeze. 'Just a temporary fix,' Mam had called it. 'Until he has more time.'

Daniel. He was temporary too. Even if he didn't know it. Mam would see sense once Dad was allowed to come home. She had to.

Billie's eyes were still sleep heavy, but she couldn't snuggle down under the covers; wouldn't sleep again. Not today. Today, Daniel was *bringing the last of his things over*.

Moving in.

He'd crept in, bit by bit over the last six months: a thief in the night, stealing the spaces that belonged to Dad. He'd brought his loud laugh that bounced off the walls, making Billie's ears hurt and the rooms too small; his eyes that pinned Mam's feet to the floor and stole her smiles.

1

But now, today, it was official. A new start, Mam had said, in a voice that wasn't hers.

Moving on . . .

Without Dad. Without telling him. Without even asking Billie.

Old Mam, *before Daniel* Mam, would never have done that.

Everything was different. Everything was wrong. Billie needed to act.

Today.

She drew her duvet around her body like a cape. She knelt up on the bed, pulled away the stupid tape and peered out through the cold, dark glass. She craned her neck, searched for stars; counted.

One.

Two.

Three.

She wiped away the breath clouds she'd made, spied another star winking above the Carlton flats. Four stars was *good*. The most she'd seen at one time here above the estate, where the sky was hardly ever clear, was never properly dark. *A hopeful sky story*, Dad would say: the promise of a still, bright day to come. Good. At least the weather was on her side.

She thought of another, remembered sky. A boot-black Dales sky scattered with silver-stud stars. Thousands of them, glittering above shadowed hills and valleys, silver waterfalls and wandering stone walls. She saw morning ravens, rising with the sun, dark and mysterious above misted hills. Had she *actually* seen all that when she was small, or had Dad painted sky pictures in her mind? She wasn't sure.

She thought of Dad. Was he awake too? Probably. She tried to picture him in his narrow bed. In his tiny, square room with no window. She wondered about a world that stole stars and the sky stories from people, just because they made one mistake. She thought again of Daniel, who never even noticed the stars, never listened to the sky. Daniel, who'd arrive as the moon slid into sleep, wanting food, quick-snap. Wanting silence.

Why did everything have to be about him? It wasn't even his home. It would never be his home.

Well, today, Billie was leaving; going to find Dad. She'd be out of the flat before Daniel got in, whatever Mam had to say about it. She'd planned to wait until he was sound asleep after his nightshift, so that she could get ready to leave; grab what she needed without worrying he might appear at any moment. She couldn't face another breakfast with a tired, cross Daniel; she wasn't spending one more tiptoe-tense morning with Mam hovering like an anxious bee in case she made too much noise while he settled off to sleep. And anyway, a four-star night sky meant a clear, frosty dawn. One of Dad's *stardust dawns*. Billie wasn't missing that.

She pulled on a T-shirt, two jumpers, jeans and thick socks. She pulled her backpack from the back of her wardrobe. It was already heavy, stuffed with blanket, old camping groundsheet, torch, spare jeans, and jumper. A chocolate bar sneaked from Daniel's stash in the fridge. And there was still food and her water bottle to add. Billie would manage, though. She had to.

She waited for the sound of Mam's quick feet, the click of the bathroom light. She headed for the kitchen and squeezed two packets of crisps and a lump of cheese into her bag. It wasn't enough, but it would have to do. She couldn't risk Mam noticing food was missing straightaway. And anyway, there was no more room. Her bag was stuffed to bursting. Billie had to hope that Mam didn't notice that either. Then again, Mam didn't notice much these days. Unless it was something to do with Daniel.

Billie had the kettle whistling on the stove and four pieces of bread in the toaster when Mam came into the kitchen, eyes sleep-squinting in the yellow stare of the fluorescent light.

'Sit down, Mam,' she said, setting mugs down on the bench. 'Tea and toast coming.'

'You're a sweetheart, Billie,' Mam said. She delved inside her dressing-gown pocket for a hair clip, gathered and twisted her dark hair; secured it on top of her head. Two tendrils sprang free. She pushed them behind her ears. 'I'll drink it while I get on.' She glanced at the wall clock. 'Bacon and eggs, as it's Saturday. Want to help?'

Billie shook her head. 'I don't eat bacon. You don't eat bacon. But, what? *Daniel* likes it, so suddenly *you* do?'

'Billie, love,' Mam sighed. Her shoulders sagged. She heaved open the cutlery drawer. Knives, forks and spoons clattered on to the table. Mam arranged them, spaced them carefully into three place settings.

The toast popped up in the toaster. Billie grabbed two pieces, spread them with butter. The scrape of the knife was too loud. She handed Mam a mug of tea. Steam curled from the rim, disappeared into the morning-cold room.

'Anyway, Mam, I'm going out,' she said. 'To collect leaves and stuff. For school.'

It was mainly true. She needed leaves for a winter art project. She just didn't need them yet.

5

Mam glanced at the wall clock. 'It's early to be going out, Billie. Dark still.'

Billie shrugged. 'Better than staying here,' she muttered.

Mam sat down on the edge of the wooden chair – a butterfly touching down, ready to flit. She wrapped her hands around her mug, searched Billie's face. She twirled a finger around one of Billie's curls.

'Give Daniel a chance, eh, love? Things *will* get easier – better – for both of us with him here: *properly* here, as part of the family. You'll see.' She looked away, stared down into her tea and swirled it like she was searching for something there. Like maybe she didn't believe what she'd just said either.

Like maybe a bit of Old Mam was still there, just behind her eyes.

She must be able to see it now, after six months of having him around. Daniel wasn't going to make anything better for anyone. Except himself. And he didn't want to be a part of anything. He just wanted to take over, be in charge.

It was worth one more try. Billie touched Mam's hand. It felt cold, dry as a discarded autumn leaf.

'Tell him, Mam, *please*. Tell him you've changed your mind about him. That you don't want him to move in;

don't want *him* any more. You can't do. He doesn't even make you laugh like he used to. Doesn't let you be *you* any more. Not really. And he . . . he hates me . . .'

Billie's breath stilled.

Mam was still. Completely still.

Was she listening for once?

Billie threw her last hopes out into the still air.

'Anyway, you *can't* let Daniel move in *now*! Dad's due out soon and you haven't even told him, have you? How's he going to feel when he finds Daniel here? He won't let him stay. *We're* still a family – me, you, and Dad. It can be just like it was before . . . before everything. Remember?' Billie watched Mam's face, tried to read it. Couldn't. It was . . . closed.

She bit her lip, carried on. '*Dad*'ll make things better, Mam, he'll put things right. You know he will. He'll get a job again and you won't have to work so hard or worry about money. We'll be able to move, get away from this flat and go somewhere that doesn't feel sad and heavy and – boxed-in. You still love Dad, I know you do. You *have* to. He's still the same person, still the same *Dad* . . .'

Mam sighed, looked up at Billie. She opened her mouth to say something, shook her head. The clock hands clunked, punctured the silence. Seven a.m.

7

Mam squeezed Billie's hand, pushed herself up from the table as if her own body – or her lost words – were weighing her down. She reached for the frying pan and olive oil; opened a box of eggs.

'We've been through this, Billie,' Mam said. 'Daniel and me – how things are – it's complicated. But we're fine.' She smiled at Billie – the new straight-line smile that didn't reach her eyes. 'I know it's hard for you to understand, love. Especially with your dad . . .'

She cracked an egg against the side of a bowl. The stringy contents clung to its jagged edges, hung in mid-air like they didn't want to leave the protection of the shell.

'What? *With my dad* what?'

'With him being – *deciding* – to be out of touch these last months.'

She turned, threw the eggshell into the pedal bin. The lid snapped shut.

A pain shot through Billie's chest. It was true. Not a word from Dad for nearly eleven months. Not even on her birthday. Mam didn't seem to care about that either; hadn't even tried to find out why. Billie had. She'd telephoned the prison herself, but no one wanted to tell *her* anything. They'd just said she should talk to her mam . . .

Mam took scissors from the drawer, cut a strip of white

fat from a rasher of bacon. Daniel didn't like fat. She glanced at the clock again.

'You go on out then, love; get those leaves,' she said, lifting her voice; trying to sound like the other mam. The one that never ate bacon. The one that smiled at Billie and Dad under their special tree like her whole world was there on that patch of grass. The one that listened.

Billie stared down at the table, fiddled with the knives and forks. Parts of her face flitted and flickered back at her from the shiny steel surfaces. As if pieces of *her* – thin, jumbled shards of her – were caught here, scattered on the red plastic cloth. Her heart ached.

'No further than the play park, mind,' Mam added over her shoulder. 'And remember what I've said about Tanglewood: just the very edge. No further. Back for lunch, twelve thirty sharp. OK?'

That was it then. Mam was *actually* doing this. Actually replacing Dad with Daniel. Billie's last hopes of her seeing sense drifted away like steam from the kettle. At least she'd forgotten her worries about how early Billie was leaving. Daniel and his on-time breakfast trumped everything.

Even Billie's broken heart.

Well, she wasn't staying one more minute under the same roof as him. Wasn't being any part of Mam's 'new

9

family'. She *had* to do something. About Daniel. About Mam – keeping her safe.

About Dad.

'I know, Mam,' she said, fingers crossed behind her back. 'No further than the edge of the wood – and see you lunchtime then.'

She slid her bag from under the chair, took a large bite of toast and chewed hard, afraid that a twitch of her mouth might give away the lie.

That was another bad thing that had arrived with Daniel. Needing to lie to Mam.

That, and the loud silences any time Billie mentioned Dad.

TWO

The streetlamps were still on when Billie left the flat. Yellow pools on icing-white pavements. A breath-cloud and frost-diamond beautiful dawn, just as the sky story had promised. Bone-freezing in her 'winter' coat, though. Especially at this hour. But it was cold indoors anyway, would feel colder once Daniel was there. Indoor cold had sharp-glass edges and trapped her words in her throat. Outdoor cold was kinder. Even at seven in the morning. Outdoors was freedom. Especially today.

Early works traffic hummed in the distance. A car engine spluttered and surged into life somewhere nearby. Billie walked on. She painted finger-frost trails along the sides of still sleeping cars; snap-cracked ice in the gutter with her boots; tried to pretend this was a winter Saturday in her other life. The one where she was happy and looking forward to Christmas with Mam and Dad. The one before Dad made his BIG MISTAKE and Mam met Daniel.

The one where Billie wasn't running away.

A light flipped on in Garston Block as she walked past: a splash of life among rows of dead-eye windows. Billie looked up. The moon was tired now; the last of its pale light picking out the flat roofs and hard grey edges of the estate. If Billie hurried, she'd have time for an hour of watching the slide of winter sun through trees, of listening to the sounds – the *symphony*, Dad would call it – of the waking wood. She always felt close to him in Tanglewood, even though he had never been there. He would love it, Billie knew. It might not have the forever skies, the great sweeping hills and soaring birds of his beloved Dales, but Tanglewood was full of the wild, ancient songs and scents of the earth that were part of him. Part of them both.

And best of all, ravens lived there.

Today, she'd need to venture further in than she had before. Further than Mam wanted. Far enough to be hidden.

She'd be fine. She doubted she'd be able to get *too* far in anyway. Dense tangles of trunks, leafless vines and bushes twisted together beyond the first few rows of conifers and birch. Billie's new classmates whispered about witches and ghosts that lurked there; hidden in the dense growth. They clawed their hands and bared their teeth, made eerie calls; called the clusters of black crows and ravens that lined the trees there 'harbingers of evil'. A sign of 'dark forces'. A warning. Even the adults were nervous of the wood. They swapped stories of dogs disappearing after venturing too deep in pursuit of enticing scents. Down to the ravens, likely, some said; *merciless killers*, they called them. Others talked of 'strangers' lurking there, *up to goodness knows what*.

All nonsense. Had to be. Billie had never seen anyone hanging around Tanglewood other than some annoying kids from school. And anyway, it wasn't woods or birds or stupid, made-up stories that were scary. *Home* was scary. *Mam* was disappearing, and Billie felt herself shrinking a little bit more every day that Daniel was there, and Dad was . . . nowhere.

The Tanglewood ravens were just ravens. They belonged in the wood. It was their home. Round here, in this concrete and brick estate, they had nowhere else to go. They clustered together in their tree tower blocks. Like the people in their piled-high flats. Like Billie and Mam. And Daniel. Were the birds happy there, Billie wondered?

She thought back to her own first weeks in the flat last winter – *their* first weeks: just Billie and Mam. She'd hated the estate; hated their new home on principle. It didn't have Dad in it. Or any of his things. She'd hated that she could smell Mrs Daley's boiled cabbage in the hallway every Sunday, mixing with the ever-present spices that scented their landing and drifted down the stairwell. Hated the way old Mr Lavinski stuck his head out of his doorway every time she set foot outside her own. He was probably just lonely, she knew, and wanting to talk to someone. Anyone. But she never knew what to say.

When they'd first arrived, she'd especially hated the night-time blend of other people's music and TVs invading her bedroom – a muddle of thumps and whines and wobbling voices that didn't fit together in her head; made her feel further and further away from home. From Dad. But she'd got used to them. A bit. And then, just as the June sun was warming things, bringing the flutter of bright curtains to grey windows, moving the noise *out*side and gentler air *in*side, Mam had met Daniel. *Daniel*, with his silences and his ice-cold stares that built walls between Billie and Mam. His shouting that kept Billie awake at night, glued her feet to the floor during the daytime. Since then, Billie had felt glad, sometimes, to have noises from other lives to block out the sounds of her own. And she preferred outside to inside more than ever.

But this new outside had hardly any green. She would never get used to that.

Their old, boxy house over the other side of town had been cramped; all dark colours and bobbled wallpaper that crept through Mam's fresh pastel paint in places *like they had to have the last word*, she'd say. Dad had never managed to replace the threadbare carpets inherited from the last tenants; never had the money to make it happen. But 12 Lambert Drive had a *garden*: narrow and long: a back lawn threaded with wildflowers that changed colour with the seasons and hummed with insects in the spring and summer. And trees. Two of them: a bent old cherry tree that brought pink snowdrifts in May, and a tall, graceful fir tree that held birds' nests in spring and sheltered them from sharp northern winds in winter.

Dad had insisted that the lawn be left wild; had laid stepping stones through the middle. He'd mown just a small, square patch under the cherry tree, where he and Billie could lie on a blanket, read the sky stories together, and listen to the chatter of birds in the waving conifer. Search for stars.

In warm weather, Mam had joined them, smiling and sleepy, a book resting on her chest. That patch of lawn had felt like the centre of the universe.

An ice chip of longing stung Billie's heart. Was their small universe still there at number 12, or overgrown;

neglected? Obliterated by concrete paving stones or pebbles? She couldn't bear it. They never should have left it behind. When they did, Billie and Mam had floated away somewhere; lost in starless space.

Billie sighed. Her feet dragged, heavy-slow. She understood that money had been tighter with Dad no longer contributing. She'd worried about Mam taking on a second job, worried about the shadows under her eyes and the new flat notes in her voice. She'd hated that everyone had whispered about them – about Dad – behind their hands. In school. In the local shop. They had no right. Didn't know *anything*. But still, she didn't see why she and Mam had to move from their home – *Dad*'s home – and end up in this stupid tower-block flat, without even a window box of flowers for the insects. With not one tree visible from its narrow windows. With barely a single bird visitor and hardly any stars.

Mam said the flat was easier for work. Cheaper to keep. And Billie could have a fresh start in a new school, where nobody need know anything about them – about Dad, unless she wanted them to. *In the end, they'd just have to get on with it*, Mam had said. *Thanks to your dad . . .*

And Billie *had* been getting on with it – doing her best, anyway. Even though somehow, *everyone* seemed to know *everything* about them by the end of the first month. *Especially* the kids at school. And here she had no friends at all to stick up for her.

She'd just kept her head down, waited for Dad to come home and make everything better. She'd been counting down the days . . .

But then came Daniel, and with him, the realisation that she, Billie, was the only one that wanted things how they used to be. The only one that wanted Dad home.

What your dad did, Billie. It changed things between us. Surely you can understand. I need to build a new life for myself. For us. And Daniel, well, Daniel is the start of that . . .

Billie hadn't understood. And she never would. She didn't want a new life. She wanted her old one back. The one where she and Dad were together.

Until that happened, she'd looked for Dad out under the sky that still stretched between them; still connected them, even though he could hardly ever see it any more. In the few city trees that reached towards it; in the few birds that soared above the town and made it their home.

She'd found the woods the first time Daniel had *brought a few things over* so he could stay for a whole *weekend* at their new flat. Perhaps she had set out to find it without realising. Perhaps it had been calling to her all along . . .

It had been right at the end of an afternoon of keeping out of the way; of unexpected late August heat that seared her pale skin and scattered new freckles across her nose. The sun had glared down at her, as furious and unforgiving as she'd felt inside. The pooling shadows underneath the summer trees had been irresistible, despite the whispered tales that floated into her mind when she'd realised: this must be Tanglewood.

Hovering on the edge that day, watching the shadow play of leaves, the flash of spun-gold sunlight through the branches, Billie had spotted a blackbird in the silver arms of a birch – orange beak wide, chest swelling with song. She'd stepped forward, felt a welcome from the wood, as if it had been waiting for her all along.

Then she'd seen the ravens. And Dad's voice had come to her, as pure and clear and real as the blackbird's song. She'd felt him there with her, staring up at the dark-suited raven chorus line, their deep *cronk* adding bass notes to the blackbird's treble voices. Maybe they were warning notes: this was nesting time and ravens were territorial birds, Billie knew. They'd been known to fly at intruders who came too close. *Just defending their young, Billie, that's all*, she heard Dad say. *And their territory. What's left of it.*

People shouldn't blame them for that, but they do. We're the invaders, after all: we human beings, edging out their natural homes with our towns and cities, our roaring motorways . . .

'An unkindness of ravens', that's the collective term for a group of them. So unfair. Their harsh cry doesn't help, I suppose, or the fact that they feed on dead things and bother the farmers at lambing time. People find them frightening, assume they're bad news. But they're doing no more than any other wild creature, trying to survive. You should see them out in the Dales, Billie-Blue – way out in the hills and valleys, swooping and soaring on the air currents like the great raptors they are. Beautiful birds, Billie. Mysterious birds with rainbows on their wings. Clever birds, just made for stories . . .

The Tanglewood ravens had let Billie be since that first day, sometimes calling to one another in their watchtower trees, sometimes still and silent and solid. They became like friends. Little pieces of Dad, who loved all birds, but the majestic, misunderstood raven most of all . . .

Over the months, the raven numbers in Tanglewood had dwindled; family-building done for the year, Billie supposed. But there were always a few, hunched guardians of the evergreens at the opening to the wood. And Billie's heart always lifted when she saw them there.

These days, their wood was the only place she felt at home. The one place she felt truly safe. Tanglewood, with its soft snaps and creaks and wind-whispers and sweet songs. Tanglewood with its space for life.

Space for Billie.

Space for Billie and Dad. He was always around her there. If she squeezed her eyes tight shut she could almost see him there. She could watch the ravens and hear his raven tales: Noah, on his ark, sending out a raven to look for dry land. The trusted raven scouts of Norse god Odin, bringing him news from far and wide. The queen's ravens, wings clipped so that they never leave the Tower of London lest Britain may fall. King Arthur, magically transformed into a raven and not really dead at all . . .

But today, there was no time for stories. Today, Billie needed to hide. And to think. Tanglewood would help her do both.

She stuffed her cold-nipped hands in her pockets and sped up again; careful not to stumble on the slip-slide pavements in her eagerness to reach the wood. She reached the empty precinct, turned the corner by the chip shop. She glanced in through the lit windows. Mr Chatterjee was already in, lifting the silver lids of his chip fryers. They glowed orange-bright and friendly behind the still-locked door; made Billie's stomach feel hollow after her hurried bites of toast. She wished she could call in, buy some of the golden scrapings from the bottom of the fryers, hot and crisp in a crinkly paper bag. But she didn't dare spend any of the coins in her pocket. She'd be needing them later. Sometimes, Mr Chatterjee waved her inside, gave her the scrapings, or a bag of chips, for nothing and asked kindly after her dad as he handed them over. Billie wondered who'd told him about Dad's trouble, but somehow she didn't mind that *he* knew. Today, he just raised a hand as she passed; smiled his kind smile; bent back over his work. Billie felt the prick of tears. For a moment, she wanted to push open the door with its friendly bell; to tell Mr Chatterjee she had run away: tell him everything and ask him to help. But no. He might call her mam. Or the police.

Billie had to do this by herself. She took deep breaths. The icy air filled her lungs, dulled the pinch of fear; the sting of resentment at Mam who had left her all alone.

She could do this. She *could*. She had to.

As she walked away from the tiny precinct, the pavement gave way to an uneven mix of old concrete, frozen mud and gravel. She stopped for a moment; admired a spider's web that wobbled between blades of winter grass at the edge of the pathway to the play park, its strands shimmering with frost-pearls. Then she hurried on, head down now, watching her step on the glittering ground.

The hum of morning traffic softened; receded. Spiky-topped conifers came into sight, waved at her from behind the play park, high above the shuttered community centre. Five minutes more and she'd be hidden away among them.

THREE

The bird was just sitting there, a scruffy black ball pressed against the rusty railings of the park. Its feathers were fluffed out, speckled with sequins of frost, like the rough surface of the play area and the patch of frozen earth underneath its body. It tilted its head towards her: slowly, as if its neck was stiff. It stared at her out of one blackcurrant eye. But it didn't move. Didn't fly away.

Could it fly? Billie wondered. Maybe it was a fledgling, still trying to learn. Although November would be too late for that. And it looked quite well grown, quite well-feathered.

Maybe it thought Billie a predator and was trying to make itself invisible by keeping still. Billie knew about trying to be invisible. She took two steps back, turned away; stood statue-still like she was part of the concrete world around them both. Part of the heavy sky. Not convincing in her horrid purple coat, she knew, but she tried her best.

She sneaked a look over her shoulder. The bird was still there, frozen to the spot. Hurt, maybe. Or sick?

Billie put down her rucksack and crept closer: cat-quiet, like Dad had taught her, tried to get a better look.

'It's a *raven*, Dad,' she whispered. 'I'm *sure* it is . . .'

It could sometimes be hard to tell them apart from other very young Corvids, she remembered him saying: crows and rooks especially. She squeezed her eyes shut, tried to recall the images in Dad's *Book of British Birds*. But no. This bird was thinner than it should be, perhaps, but still, judging by the size of its feet and the beginnings of a shaggy beard underneath its chin, this was *definitely* a raven.

She pictured Dad's book, hidden away on the top of her wardrobe. With the other things she'd saved from being boxed up in the garage block, trapped down with tape like they might escape.

As if Dad wouldn't be needing them again.

As if he wasn't coming home and Daniel had taken his place, like a cuckoo in someone else's nest. As if that was fine because *Dad only had himself to blame*, like Mam said.

The bird was still staring at Billie. It rocked on its twig legs, pressed its feathers close to its body like it was trying to make itself smaller; trying to disappear. Then Billie remembered: birds tightened their feathers like that in preparation for flight. Perhaps it was going to fly away after all. She would keep still; watch it go.

It lifted one wing, moved it up and down. There were patches of pink beneath it; stubby feathers poking through in places. The other wing stayed flat. Broken, perhaps.

The bird opened its hooked gunmetal beak but made no sound. It turned, stumbled away, lopsided and unsteady on its too-big feet. Like stupid Daniel, back from the King's Head with his stupid Saturday night friends, his words slurry and loud. His fists that made holes in doors and once, storm-cloud blue bruises on Mam's wrist. Mam said she'd caught her hand in the door. But Billie knew she hadn't.

Her stomach tightened. Today was Saturday.

Mam might need her. Should she go back?

But no. She *couldn't*. Mam wasn't listening. Billie needed to get going . . . make . . . carry out her plan.

But what about the bird – the *raven*? She should at least make sure that *it* was safe before she hurried on.

She watched it totter towards the park gate, where it did a sequence of unbalanced hops. Stopped. Tried to hide around the back of a spindly tree. The only tree by the park. Its wedge-shaped tail stuck out, black against the frosted ground.

A giveaway.

Poor thing.

But perhaps its family were nearby, watching out for it, waiting for Billie to leave. A couple of adult ravens – even a single, irate mother, might scare off predators. They were large birds. Or did ravens leave their young to their own devices once they'd fledged?

Billie looked round for any sign of raven family protectors. She peered across the deserted play park with its tall slide and broken swing-frame, checked the roof of the old community centre. They glared back at her, ghostly white. Empty. She scanned the sky. Nothing but the pasty face of the moon hovering above the rooftops in its slide into sleep, the telegraph wires stretching across the faded-ink air.

Then she was seeing Dad. Seeing his face as he pointed up at black-dot birds perched shoulder to shoulder on the wires. Musical notes on the page. She heard his voice, special-soft: *Bird music, Billie! See? Birds writing their beautiful songs for you, right there in the sky!*

She looked away.

No bird notes now.

No more music.

No more Dad.

The ice chip shifted, needle sharp.

Billie brushed her gloved hand across her eyes. The wool was soggy on her cold cheeks. She blinked, stared down at the bird. It blurred at the edges: an ink-black smudge on white paper.

What could she do for it? What *should* she do? Her white breath curled on the air. She watched it drift and disappear. Dad's voice came again, echoing around her head from somewhere that felt long ago and right now both at the same time. For a moment, he was there, standing next to her, his field-green eyes gentle. *Wild things belong to the wild, Billie-Blue. They don't do well anywhere else. Best leave them be. Leave them free.*

But if this bird was injured, or ill, it wouldn't survive long in the wild – Billie knew that much. It was all alone. Helpless. If the cold didn't finish it off, the skinny estate cats would. In a heartbeat. And they were everywhere, lurking in wait for an easy meal.

Kids too. Mean kids like Jimmy and Shannon Blythe, with cheap November fireworks in their pockets, sticks in their hands, and nothing much to do but look for someone – or some*thing* – to pick on. They hung around the play park on weekends and after school too. They liked messing about on the edge of the wood. Throwing stones up into the trees, laughing at the startled birds and occasional scampering squirrel. Billie couldn't understand them. How would they like stones thrown at *their* homes?

She glanced over her shoulder again; looked back at the path from the estate. No sign yet of Shannon and her crew. They'd still be in their beds. But the helpless bird couldn't be here when they did turn up.

Perhaps, if it would let her pick it up, Billie could take it into the wood. Away from the edge. It could hide there, be sheltered from the worst of the cold among the evergreens; tuck itself away in a tree hollow until it felt stronger. Then it could balance high in the bare oaks, scan the wood for its bird family. Surely, they would be there. Birds like this didn't migrate for the winter. And there was nowhere else to go round here: just the brick and cement and concrete constructions that had eaten away at their leafy homes. Only Tanglewood remained. And, according to Mr Chatterjee, it was growing smaller by the year.

Billie decided. She hadn't been able to stop Daniel. She hadn't been able to make Mam listen. Not yet. But she could do something right now for this helpless bird.

Leave wild things free, Billie-Blue.

'I've got to do *something*, Dad,' she said into the empty air.

28

She took a breath; soft-sneaked towards the spindly tree hideout. The black tail trembled. 'Don't worry,' she whispered. 'Don't run away. I'm going to help you.'

The bird squatted low; shuddered, sank into the ground a little more. For all it knew, Billie was as cruel as a narrow-eyed cat moving in for the kill. Should she keep talking to it, she wondered, make soothing noises, or would that frighten it even more?

Best just get it over with.

She expected the bird to try to escape again when she knelt close. It didn't. She moved her hands towards it, closed them slowly around its body, brought it up to her chest.

It was light. Much lighter than it looked. Like she had captured a cloud. A cloud with a hammer-heart thudding through her gloved hands. She stared down, as fright-frozen as the creature she was holding. The wind parted the short feathers on the top of its head. It didn't struggle. Only pecked at her glove. Just once. As if it knew there was no point but had to try. A tuft of fluff hung from its beak, red as blood, and floated away on the breeze.

Billie pulled off her hat and eased it around the bird, terrified she might crush its bones with even the tiniest bit of pressure. She balanced the woolly bundle in the crook of her elbow, jiggled down the zip of her coat with one hand. For once, she was grateful for her embarrassingly large charity-shop coat – bought for her to 'grow into'. At least it had room to spare. She snuggled the bird in its knitted nest against her jumper, pulled off her glove with her teeth, closed the coat zip almost to the top. She bit her lip, moved the zip down another couple of centimetres in case the bird needed more air.

She felt a tremble against her heart; a sliver of warmth through the woollen layers covering her chest.

'Just ten minutes, bird,' she whispered, 'and you'll be home.'

FOUR

Billie stood at the entrance to the woods. Bare branches of birch and oak spread like lace against the lightening sky. On a topmost branch, two crows balanced; swayed gently in the breeze: high-wire experts on their impossibly thin perch.

Billie listened. There it was: the breathy whisper of wind through fir tree and evergreen; the rustle of winter-crisp leaves on the forest floor. The forest was speaking – telling its winter stories, singing its winter songs.

Billie undid her coat a little, so that the bird could listen too; could pick up the earthy scents of home. She stayed rock-still, captivated; her worries somehow part of another world, another Billie that didn't exist in this place. Tanglewood was extra beautiful today. Spangles of dawn light danced through the tree canopy, lit sparks across the reds, conker-browns and golds of the autumn leaf-carpet. Frost sparkled like stardust across it. Across everything. Dad's stardust dawn. Billie felt the sparks – the stardust –

inside herself too. Tiny darts of happiness. She loved this winter wood.

She looked down at the bird. The bird looked back.

Where would be best to release it? Where might be safe enough? She looked around, eyes following the rough pathway that had been trampled amid these first rows of trees. She had followed it for a few minutes when she first discovered Tanglewood. It snaked around the perimeter for a while, then came to an abrupt stop. It was no use going that way this time. They needed to go deeper inside the wood, away from the pathway, away from the eyes and reach of kids with stones and stalking cats.

Deeper than Billie had been before.

'We'll just go a *bit* further in, OK, bird?' she whispered.

Sorry, Mam, she thought.

The bird blinked. Quivered. Was it excited to be back in the wild wood, or just sick and scared? Billie wished she knew. But she shouldn't keep hold of it any longer than necessary. Needed to find that safe place for it to rest and recover. Which way was best? Left, right or straight ahead?

There was no way of knowing.

She wrapped her arms around herself, around the bird bundle, and stepped away from the beaten track. She pushed straight ahead, past deep green holly bushes, careful of the pin-sharp leaves that guarded scarlet berries. She squeezed between thin silver-black birch trunks that reached into the sky like ancient pillars. She brushed against gnarled oaks looped with creepers – some dried-out and leafless, wound tight like strangling snakes. Others – some kind of ivy – trembled as Billie passed. Their glazed leaves glistened like tiny stars where strobes of early winter sun caught them.

Spaces narrowed as Billie walked. Twigs snatched at her coat sleeves. Roots rose from the ground and tumbled over one another, some camouflaged by the leaf-carpet. Billie had to watch her step. It was almost as if Tanglewood was trying to keep her out: the trees and bushes leaning inwards, barring her way, thrusting their limbs up through the earth to hinder her. But no. She wasn't going to think like that. It was just an ancient wood, left to ramble as it should. It was *her* wood. And if scary stories and dense growth kept kids like Shannon and Jimmy away, then good. Good for the wood and everything that lived here ...

She pushed on; eyes peeled for a safe, snug refuge for the trembling bird and a girl that needed to hide. The trees and bushes pressed more and more tightly against one another as she walked. Branches and twigs knitted together overhead, like linked arms and interlocking fingers. They made a kind of roof. There was shelter here from the worst of the wind; spaces in the tree roof for warming needles of winter sun.

This might be a good spot. Billie stopped; looked around, hoping, first of all, to spot a tree-hollow hideout for the bird.

There was an old tree stump, the middle eaten away – by ants, perhaps. It made a kind of leaf-strewn cradle. No. That was too low to the ground to be safe. Billie turned in a slow circle. To her left, a few paces ahead, the woodland colours were changed: richer, brighter. She wriggled and ducked in that direction.

A broad shaft of light pushed between the trees, lit a kind of doorway between two ancient oaks. Billie stooped, edged her way under low-set branches. Morning bird music lifted in the air; grew louder.

Billie's bird squawked – a first sound. An answering call, perhaps. Did it know this place? She peered inside her coat. The black bead eyes stared up at her.

Another squawk – small, uncertain. What was the bird saying?

'Is this the place?' Billie whispered. 'Do you belong here?'

The bird looked away, tucked its head low; was silent. Billie would have to work this out by herself.

She picked her way between the thick roots of the oaks; stepped through the tree doorway. She gasped.

She was in a clearing. A wide, circular clearing, enclosed by tall trunks and tangled bushes that seemed to have shuffled, shoulder to shoulder to form a wall. The leaf-carpet here was thick and bright. It rose up as she moved, covered her toes: a red and gold wave. The shaft of light that had drawn Billie here fell like a spotlight in the centre of the clearing. Frost diamonds and tiny insects danced inside it.

And there, impossibly – hanging from an outstretched oak arm: a swing.

A wooden swing-seat suspended on thick ropes.

Billie froze. Who had put it there? It looked a little weathered, the seat fading, the straw-coloured ropes greying. But it didn't look *really* old. It didn't look forgotten.

Who else came here? Were they here now, watching her? She scanned the clearing.

A scuffle among the bushes.

Billie jumped. Her heart thudded under the bird-bundle in her coat.

A flash of rust-red at the side of a silver birch.

A quick-dash-flick of russet tail . . .

A squirrel. That was all.

Billie watched it leap from branch to branch, tree to tree – an autumn acrobat, quickly out of sight within a deep green fir. Billie breathed out. The bird wriggled and squirmed.

Right. Where should she settle him? She needed to focus . . .

The squirrel's evergreen refuge had a wide skirt of thickly fringed branches, some low to the ground. Billie squatted on her haunches, peered underneath them. They created a kind of shaded awning, high enough at some points for her to stand. Light flickered there. Leaf shadows danced. The tree trunk was vast: wide and ancient, full of knots and crevices. A tree for climbing. And for hiding in. She cradled her bird-bundle against her chest and scrambled inside the tree tent.

A blackbird darted up from the ground, a worm dangling from its orange beak. A robin peered at her from a fallen branch, head on one side, hopped further away and pecked at the leaf-carpet.

'What do you think, bird?' she whispered into her coat. 'Looks like there's plenty of food for you here. And company too.'

The bird wriggled again, flicked more red wool from its beak in a kind of bird-sneeze. It blinked up at Billie. It seemed more alive now. Perhaps she should try putting it down, see what happened. It might hop away this time, choose its own hiding place. It might even fly, here in the safety of the woodland.

But as soon as she slid her hands around it, the bird froze. Again, the drumbeat heart through her gloves. She peeled back the hat from its ink-black feathers; had to unloop a thread from one of its clawed toes. They were long, curved and sharp: made Billie think of the hawks and eagles in Dad's book, prey grasped beneath them as they swooped through the sky, ancient – *prehistoric* – echoes of long-dead dinosaur ancestors in the spread of their wings.

Dad. She needed him here with her *right now*. Why had he stopped writing? The need for him ached, opened up an empty-sky space in her chest. Like some great pterosaur had swooped down and ripped away a piece of her heart. How could Dad not feel the same? Had his heart turned grey and stiff and solid like the prison walls; pressed the memory of Billie and Mam deep inside where he couldn't reach it? Where it didn't hurt.

Billie drew a ragged breath. *Not now*, she told herself.

She steadied her breathing; lowered the bird into a dip on the fallen branch. The bark there was softened, green-brown with moss and lichen. A soft place to land. She stepped back. Waited.

The bird fluffed out its feathers, hunkered down. Trembled. It wouldn't move with her there. Of course it wouldn't. She ducked underneath the edge of the tree-awning, crouched behind one of the silver guardians of the clearing, where she could catch glimpses of the bird as the sugar-frosted fir fronds moved in the breeze.

The bird was still.

Billie waited. Watched.

The bird was still.

The light shifted, became stronger. Her legs grew stiff. Pins and needles prickled in the left one. She would have to stand up now. And anyway, she needed to get on. Winter days were short and she needed to get further away, find an overnight hideout for herself once she'd settled the bird.

As she moved, the bird called. Or, at least, she thought it did. Could it have been another bird?

She peeped in between the fir-tree fingers. The bird opened its beak wide, called in a strange squawking cry that nipped at Billie's heart. It looked so small, so alone, there amid the towering, tangled trees. She longed to scoop it back into the hat-nest; to comfort it if she could. But perhaps it was calling for its family. If so, she needed to keep out of sight, or they'd never come near.

The cries grew louder. No bird rescue party appeared. But who else might? Who else might see the young bird as a tasty lunch? Billie swallowed. The poor thing was still in danger. She hadn't helped it at all. She crawled under the tree-skirt, kept her body low; sat, chin on her knees, close enough to guard it while she decided what to do next.

The bird decided for her. It shuffled forward, flopped down from its branch perch, did its awkward, stumbling dance in Billie's direction. It stopped a few paces away. Its beak opened. It squawked, louder this time: its voice too big somehow; off key. Billie knew those bird notes. Recognised them inside herself. The bird had called for its family, and they hadn't come.

Was it now calling for *her*, or just panicking? Either way, she couldn't just leave it on the forest floor.

She knelt in front of it, pulled her hat from her pocket and gently scooped it back inside. This time, it didn't react. Maybe it had given up – like the baby rabbit she once saw on the roadside, eyes closed in surrender as three large birds sauntered towards it. Crows. Billie had hidden her face in her dad's coat, begged him to save the little creature and let her take it home as a pet. He had shooed the birds away, carried the shivering rabbit to the shelter of the hedgerow. Left it in the wild. Where it belonged. Where it might be the next meal for a hungry bird. Or a fox. Billie had cried; told him he was mean and cruel too. She felt his hand now, feather-soft on her cheek, saw his field-green eyes, crinkle-kind at the corners. *It's the way of things, Billie. The way everything works together in nature. Those crows, they're just doing what they need to do to stay alive; to feed their families.*

The great talons gripped tighter around her heart, as if to pull it from its roots. Bold black newspaper print danced before her eyes: '*I WAS JUST TRYING TO FEED MY FAMILY*' – LOCAL MAN GUILTY OF THEFT FROM EMPLOYER.

Dad's words. Stolen and spilled across the local paper for all to see. They seemed to bounce off the trees now; to surround her, like the voices in the playground that terrible week. Closing in with their questions; their nudges and whispers. She thought again of the small rabbit; the circling crows.

Mam had said their house move was a blessing; that she'd be free of all that nonsense in her new school. That nobody would know about Dad. She'd been wrong.

She had known that first morning, even as she waved to Mam at the gate. The pointing fingers in the playground. The staring in the classroom.

The other 'newbies' or friendless few that attached themselves to the 'new girl' then drifted away like mist before the end of the first week as if Billie smelled of something really bad.

The town library had back copies of local papers, she discovered. Marley Blake's mam worked there. And Billie had an unusual surname . . .

And then there was the internet. And Sita Patel's big sister, who, according to Sita, *could find out everything about everybody on there.*

Mam had spoken to the teacher, of course. There'd been an assembly about 'kindness' and 'caring for others in our school'. But Billie had kept herself to herself from that first week on. She was pretty sure everyone hated her even more because of that. Even her hair was the wrong colour now – as if the flame-red wildness of it marked her out somehow.

Different. Wild. Not to be trusted. Just like her dad . . .

The clearing felt suddenly small, like the trees were closing in too.

Billie didn't want to be there any more.

The bird made a sudden flutter-hop inside her hat. It stared at her, light darting across its eyes. It began to tremble again. Billie chewed at her bottom lip. What on earth was she going to do? The little creature looked so weak. Thin and cold. However afraid of her it was, it seemed to know that it couldn't survive out here by itself. It needed looking after, some warmth and company and proper meals, whatever that meant for a young raven. But Billie couldn't care for it out in the winter wood – she barely had enough food for herself, wasn't even sure she could keep herself warm enough overnight, let alone a sick bird. Tomorrow, she'd need to move on, go to the prison or something, or she might not survive either. Her heart flutter-hopped like the bird. There was only one thing for it. Her own plans – her escape plans would have to wait just a tiny bit longer. She drew in a deep breath, blinked back the burn of tears.

'Come on then, bird,' she said. 'You'd better come home with me. But just for a bit. Just till you feel better.' She eased it back inside the hat-nest. This time, it didn't put up a fight. She wasn't sure if that was a good sign or not. She snuggled it back inside the dark safety of her coat.

Home.

Billie checked her watch. Eleven thirty. If she hurried, she could still make Mam's lunch deadline. Keep her happy. Keep Daniel happy.

Her stomach tightened and twisted. Daniel. Saturday Daniel. She'd have to see him again after all. He would be there now, back from his nightshift. Could she smuggle the bird inside the flat without him knowing she had come in? She might if he was already sleeping. But if he had the weekend off, like he sometimes did, he might stay up for a while. Then he'd be in the kitchen with Mam. Billie's face grew hot at the thought of him sitting in Dad's chair like he owned it, or hovering around Mam, picking fault as she sweated over steaming pans.

Mam *might* not hear Billie come in, especially if the radio was turned up loud like it normally was when Daniel was around. But Daniel. Daniel noticed everything. If he *was* there, he'd call Billie into the kitchen as soon as he heard the front door. Just because he could.

And Daniel didn't like birds. *Filthy, flapping things, birds. Vermin, the lot of them. Can't stand 'em.*

He'd tutted at Billie's bird posters, told her to take them down. Told Mam she should *step on this obsession of Billie's before she turned out as wild as her dad. Look where that got him . . .*

She hadn't taken them down. So yesterday, Daniel had. And he had tossed Dad's bird books and sketches into hideaway boxes while Billie was at school. Mam had only sighed and whispered; eyes fixed on the lounge door in case he reappeared. *Just let it go, Billie, love. Let it go. You know where they are if you want them . . .*

Billie's cheeks grew angry-hot all over again, despite the freezing air. Daniel was wiping Dad away like a dirty smear on the window, and Mam was just letting him do it.

Billie felt the pull of guilt under her ribs. She should have ripped open those boxes herself. But she hadn't. Couldn't. She'd seen the narrowing of Daniel's eyes when she opened her mouth to speak, and her traitor voice had disappeared. She'd let Dad down. She never wanted to do that again. *Wouldn't* ever do that again. Now she was going back home again, where there were more and more things that Daniel couldn't stand. Billie was pretty sure she was one of them. What would Daniel do if he found out she'd brought a bird into the flat?

She pictured his angry fists.

Furious fists that flew fast out of nowhere and for nothing.

Fists that could crush a small raven in a heartbeat. Might they then come for her?

Billie's throat tightened. She swallowed hard.

One step at a time, Billie, she thought. *One step at a*

time. Just get past Daniel to your room, that's all you have to do for now.

Her best hope was that he'd crashed out after breakfast and was snoring soundly in their room. She sent a silent wish up through the leaf canopy and into the stardust sky.

'Let's go, bird,' she whispered through her scarf. 'And don't be scared. We'll be OK. We *will*.'

She straightened her shoulders and looped her scarf low over her chest to disguise the bump there. Just in case she met someone nosy on her way home.

FIVE

There was no way of avoiding the girl. She was leaning against the play-park fence, one leg bent up behind her. Red knees between wrinkled socks and huge wellies, bright green mittens dangling from a duffle coat two sizes too small for her. It looked to Billie as though she was wearing summer shorts underneath it. She hooked her hands around the top of the railings, leaned away from them as Billie got close.

'What you got?' she said. 'Under yer coat?' She nodded towards Billie's chest, making her brown hair fall over her face. She shook it away, sniffed; stared at Billie with hazelnut-round eyes.

Billie stared back. She'd seen this girl before – hanging around the edges of the schoolyard. A new pupil, perhaps. Or another loner, like herself. They'd never exchanged a word though, and Billie wasn't interested in doing so now. She hurried on past.

'Books, is it?' the girl shouted after her.

Billie stopped, turned.

'Books?'

The girl nodded. She squinted at Billie between strands of light hair, pointed back towards a peeling green bench inside the play park, where what looked like a large picture book lay open, pages lifting in the wind like wings.

'Books from the library, like. Seen you in it lunchtime yesterday, when I were getting that 'un, there. An' the day before that.'

Billie *was* always in the library at lunchtimes. Better that than being in the playground. But it wasn't about the books. Not really. Well, the non-fiction ones perhaps: books on birds and the planets; real stuff. But not the fiction – the stories. Not any more.

'So?' she said. 'It's quiet in the library. I like quiet. I like being by myself.'

The girl was staring up into the sky, following a black-dot bird in flight. She didn't seem to have heard. She looked back at Billie's coat.

'Or maybe you got bread and nuts and stuff for the birds? Me nan's always got pockets full of them. *Got to look out for the birds in winter, our Nell*, that's what she says.' She dragged the back of her hand across her nose, sniffed again. 'We put bacon scraps out for them – in there.' She threw an arm towards the play park again. 'Birds are all right. Funny.' She grinned, showing a gap where one of her front teeth should be. She hopped, bird-like, from one foot to the other. 'Books are me favourite, though,' she said.

'Right,' Billie said. She sighed.

Why was this girl even out here on her own at this time? And why was she talking to Billie? Everyone else ignored her these days, other than for their stupid, boring jokes and jibes.

The bird squirmed. Its heart ticked fast and furious against Billie's chest. She needed to get going before the little creature died of fright. Billie needed to be tucked away in her room, away from Daniel's searching eyes, with the bird safe and warm. She needed to make a new plan.

'It's not books inside my coat,' she said. 'Or bird food. It's nothing. Just my hat. And gloves.' She turned away, walked on a few paces, glanced back over her shoulder. The girl was swinging back and forth from the railings again, watching her.

'I'm Nell,' the girl said. 'Case you didn't know. And we've got heaps of books. If you want to borrow one . . .'

'What?'

'Books.'

'You're all right.' Billie shuffled her feet. Last thing she needed was some nosy new girl following her, finding out about Bird. About things at home. About her plan to run away.

If she even thought that Billie was hiding something, soon enough other people would find out everything too. Secrets always escaped, got scattered like seed on the wind.

'Thanks, but . . .' Billie hesitated. She didn't want to be unkind. Maybe this Nell was just being friendly. But even if she could risk making friends right now, Nell didn't look like the kind of girl she would get along with, anyway. She looked childish, with her picture book, her mittens and over-sized wellies. What could they possibly have in common?

She offered Nell a small smile. 'We probably don't like the same books, that's all.'

'Well, I've got all sorts, mind,' Nell shouted. 'Off me nan.' She clambered over the railings, agile as a cat. 'Watch this,' she said.

She ran over to the slide, swooshed down in a spray of frost crystals, shot off the end and landed hard on the ground. She jumped up. Brushed herself down.

'She loves stories, Nan does,' she shouted. She spread her arms wide, like wings. 'There's whole worlds in stories, Nell, that's what Nan says. Whole worlds.' She turned, skipped towards the broken swing-frame; leaped in the air, arms reaching for the top bar. She didn't make it. She shrugged; wandered back over to Billie.

'Gotta go now,' she said. 'Lunchtime. Nan'll have me guts for garters if I'm late. See ya.' She hop-skipped off across the park, turned her head and yelled over her shoulder. 'Number twenty-four York Court. If you want to borrow a book or feed the birds, like. Bye!'

Billie watched her go, quick and light and purposeful as a sparrow. And for a moment, she felt the lightness inside herself too; remembered it. Wanted to call Nell back and hold on to it for a few seconds longer.

But as the flat came into view, worry was back – fat, cold and squirming in her stomach.

Nell and her nan could keep their stories. Real life didn't have happy endings like you found in books. The only stories that told the truth were the ones in the sky.

SIX

Billie crept up the stairwell of the flats, steadied the quivering bundle beneath her coat with one hand. It was gloomy, like always, the weak winter sun barely visible through the high, narrow windows above the stairs. She wondered for the hundredth time whether the person who built the flats couldn't afford the right size windows for the block. You needed artificial light all year round to see where you were going on the stairwell. To Billie, it felt unfriendly, miserable; like it didn't really want people there at all. It made her feel heavy inside.

Today, only one of the overhead lamps was working. The single beam threw Billie's stop-start shadow ahead of her on the grey stone steps: all hunched shoulders and lumpy arms in her padded coat. She stumbled in her hurry to get away from the echoey stairwell. She felt exposed there. Nervous. A young rabbit out in the open, scurrying for the comfort and safety of its burrow. Although the flat never felt comfortable now, thanks to Daniel. And not very safe at all.

But the bird was what mattered right now. Billie steadied her breathing; slid her hand along the cold metal banister as she climbed. She couldn't slip. Not this time.

Her footsteps were too loud: echoing; bouncing off the high ceiling above the stone stairs. The door to the landing was heavy-slow. Hard to open one-handed. It scraped and squealed against the concrete floor like an angry animal. At least it wouldn't snap shut behind Billie; wouldn't announce her arrival.

She poked her head and shoulders around it and looked out into the landing. Held her breath.

Listened.

Looked up and down the corridor.

Nobody.

No sound other than the wind whistling through the cracked pane by Mr Lavinski's; the scream of a kettle somewhere, quickly silenced. No thump and swell of Daniel's music through the doorway to number 32. She breathed out. If he was home, he must have already gone to bed. Otherwise, he'd have the radio on.

Maybe he was just in the shower. Or already sitting at the kitchen table, tapping his feet under the table – like a morse-code message telling Mam to hurry up with his food. Either should give Billie time to get the bird sorted without him noticing anything. Although you never knew anything for sure. Not with Daniel.

'Almost there, Bird,' she whispered into her coat. She tiptoed out on to the landing.

She'd forgotten the landing light. The automatic one that didn't know the difference between night and day. It was always there, waiting to catch Billie out, like a searchlight. It hummed, clicked on, yellow and blinding. Billie jumped. The bundle of bird jumped too. Panicked heartbeats in between her own. Fast. Too fast. Like a tiny ticking clock wound too far. Could a wild bird die of fright in this loud, echoey place? Maybe she *should* have left it where it was, after all.

But it had been scared there too. And all alone.

'Best get you inside,' she whispered.

She wriggled her key from her jeans pocket, slipped it in the lock. Waited.

Nothing.

The kitchen door was closed. Faint cooking smells – bacon mixed with something spicy that didn't belong to them – hung in the hall. Daniel's black coat was on the hook next to Mam's and Billie caught the hiss of the shower. She held her breath as she slipped off her shoes and tiptoed towards her bedroom. She didn't breathe out until she was sitting on her bed, her door closed, gentle-soft.

So far so good. But what now?

She had no idea.

She gazed out of her window. Dirty clouds, edged in gold. A dove-grey sky.

A memory surfaced – a story from Mam's childhood, of a frightened bird, fallen into the hearth – beating against the window like a moth in its frantic attempt to escape back into the sky. Billie knelt up, pulled her curtains closed. The bird fluttered against her chest. Or it might have been the flutter of her own heart, which was now making weird leaps.

She edged down the zip on her coat, switched on the bedside lamp; hoping it wasn't too scary-bright. One bird eye stared up at her again. The bedside lamp was reflected there, a miniature winter sun, trying to break through an an angry sky.

The one eye closed. Maybe the bird thought that if it couldn't see Billie, then she was no longer there. Or that she couldn't see *him*. Another memory tugged: a hide-and-seek chase with Mam and Dad; peeking behind the lounge curtains. Billie felt the memory in her body: the thrill of being found; whisked up high on to Dad's shoulders, legs swinging free. Felt the laughter, the lightness inside her. Like she was flying . . .

She swallowed hard, slid the zip a few notches lower, careful not to catch the ink-black feathers in the coat's scratched silver teeth. The bird shifted, trembled harder than ever. She could see both its eyes this time: now terror-tight shut. The eyelids were heavy, the skin around them bobbled like the dried lava she saw in the museum in town. Like dinosaur skin. There were spiky feather tufts underneath its dark beak, which was huge: too big for its head. Those spiky tufts were the start of the 'beard' that marked the raven out from the other members of the Corvid family. But did all Corvids eat the same thing? Wasn't there something about diets for different sorts of birds? Billie's heart did another somersault. She didn't even know what to feed this little thing. What if she gave it the wrong food? What if it wouldn't take *any* food from her because it was too scared?

And where was she going to keep it, anyway?

How was she going to help its wing to heal?

Pebbles of panic pushed their way into her throat. She couldn't do this. Not without Dad. She didn't know *anything*. Had she made a mistake bringing the bird home?

You made a choice, Billie-Blue. You're responsible now.

55

Take your time. Think it through. Dad, in the back of her head again.

Big on responsibility, your dad, Mam would say now, under her breath, like that was a bad thing.

Well, anyway, Dad wasn't here to be responsible. *Because of a choice he made.* Mam said that too. A lot. Especially since Daniel had been around.

And it was true. There was no escaping that.

It was up to Billie to see this through and to save the bird.

Its eyes opened. Just narrow slits. Petrified peep-eyes. It turned its head, clockwork-jerky; first one way and then the other. Like it was checking for an escape route from this new walled-in world. It didn't look up at Billie this time. Her heart squeezed. No wonder. She was a giant to such a small creature. A red-haired, purple-bodied monster that had captured it; taken it to her lair. It might die of fright any second. She needed to settle it somewhere quiet and dark, somewhere it could feel hidden. Safe.

Come on, Billie, think . . .

Maybe she could make a nest for it in the old shoebox that had her art stuff in. No, that wasn't deep enough. There was a cardboard box in the kitchen, she remembered, waiting for someone to fold it down for next week's recycling. Daniel had brought some more of his things round in it: CDs, videos and stuff he said Mam should watch instead of her 'daft soaps'. But if Billie took that, he'd ask where it had gone; what she wanted it for. Anyway, she didn't want anything that belonged to him.

Mam probably had something she could use. Old Mam, before 'everything', would have helped Billie. She'd have tutted at Dad, raised her eyes and muttered about this being down to him. But she'd have been smiling on the inside. She'd have produced a basket out of nowhere; a soft baby blanket Billie had no idea she'd kept. Now she'd just worry about Daniel – shoot nervous glances at him as he talked about germs and 'obsessions' and 'better things for a girl of her age to be doing'.

No, Mam couldn't know about the bird.

Billie glanced up her wardrobe.

Dad's box.

Could she? Could she even open it again, look at Dad's things, let alone move them somewhere else? She stared at the wardrobe. It stared back. The bird shivered.

Maybe it was time.

SEVEN

Billie laid the hat-nest on her bed. She wedged her pillow in front of it, in case the bird decided on a risky leap for freedom. Instead, it hunkered down low, shivering more than ever. Its breathing looked odd – jumpy and stop-start. Billie had better hurry.

She climbed on to her bedroom chair and reached on top of her wardrobe. She felt for the box. Nothing. She stretched up, tiptoe-tall, and there it was, right at the back, pressed up against the wall as if in disgrace. She didn't remember pushing it back that far, but perhaps she had. The pain of that day thudded back; the muddle of loss, disbelief and terror . . .

Dad disappearing down a dark stairwell in the courthouse, a stern-faced policewoman at his back. The shuffle and slide of papers and polished shoes. The snap of heels and briefcases. A back-slap. Like something was finished. Something was done – *well* done.

Billie had watched from somewhere behind herself,

blood rushing in her ears. It wasn't happening.

Dad would leap over the banister and make a run for it, like in one of those black and white films where everyone wore hats and raincoats and were either really good or really bad, and you could tell by their eyebrows.

Someone would burst in at the last second. There'd be a note, slowly unfolded. The judge would shake her wigged head; bang her hammer; say it was all a mistake . . .

THIS WAS NOT HAPPENING.

It *had* happened, though. The last strand of Dad's sunset-red hair had gone, sucked into the gloom of the stairwell. Billie had known what lay at the bottom. Cells. Little boxes with bars and loud noises that never went away, even at night. She'd seen that in films too.

There had been the press and the squeeze of a hand. Mam's voice whispering down a long tunnel.

'Tell them, Mam,' Billie had pleaded, her own words muffled; far away. 'Tell them!'

Mam's mouth a silent scribble. Her face snap-tight shut like the briefcases.

Billie's heart: cracked wide open like a fallen bird's egg . . .

She steeled herself. It was time. Even if it hurt to be amongst Dad's things, made her miss him more, she needed to do this.

She pictured Dad's letter, the last of his things she had held in her hand.

His last letter.

The Christmas letter with the star sketched in one corner and bright shiny word-gifts telling her he'd be standing under real stars beside her soon, free as a bird.

The letter that had lied.

Billie remembered the crunch and crinkle as she crushed it. The tiny blue nothingness of it when she unfurled her angry fist.

She glared at the box, her thoughts twisting and turning; muddled together like the Tanglewood vines, spiky and sharp. Longing cut through them like a knife. She pulled the box towards her, blew grey dust-balls from the surface, stepped down and lowered it on to the carpet. She sat back on her heels, took a slow breath in.

There should have been a ribbon. A blue ribbon. Holding it safely closed. It was missing. She stepped back up on to the chair, which wobbled as she stretched up on tiptoe; reached round with her hand. Dust tickled her nostrils, coated her hands and the cuffs of her sweatshirt. That was all there was. Dust.

She got down, angry heat in her cheeks. Someone had been in Dad's box. They must have. It was *her* box. No one had the right to touch it. *No one.*

Unless it was Mam. Maybe Mam had looked in the box; needed to remember. Billie's heart skipped a beat. Could that mean she did miss him? She did *lov*e him, after all?

But still, if *anything* else was missing . . .

She wiped her hands on her jeans, sat down next to the box, one arm resting on her duvet to safeguard the bird. She took another breath and lifted the lid, drumbeat heart loud in her ears.

Dad's gloves were still there: the pretend leather ones with the hole in the left thumb where he'd snagged it on a branch. So was the card Billie, aged six, had made for him for his birthday. He had loved it. The picture on the front had taken her ages. Stick Dad, with his enormous, lopsided grin; Stick Mam, bright red lips open as if she were laughing; Stick Billie with scribble-curls, the same red as Mam's painted laughter. Trees beside them in three shades of green – one with a tiny hole in it where Billie pressed too hard making the exact dark green for a fir tree.

The stick family were holding hands. They looked happy.

Happy had gone missing, like Dad's blue ribbon.

Like Dad.

But his binoculars were safe. The round lenses caught light from the window, winked up at Billie from the corner of the box. She ran her fingers over their smooth shiny surface, lifted them out, held them to her chest. Somehow, these binoculars *were* Dad. Dad, with his tangled sunset hair so like her own. She squeezed her eyes shut; saw him again: getting ready for that day in court; painting 'brave' into his smile. Saw the stiff grey suit and tightly knotted tie that belonged to someone else. She felt the press of his binoculars in her hand; felt him close her fingers around them, those wide-wonder eyes full of fire and water at the same time.

You watch those birds for me, Billie, if I don't come home today. And you listen for their music, out there with the wind in your hair. Then I'll hear them too. I'll feel that wind in my hair too. And I'll see you. That will be all I need.

Dad had walked towards the taxi, his steps heavy-small, like part of him was locked up – locked in – already. She saw him turn; his words blurred by the heart-waves crashing in her ears. *I'll be back for those binoculars before you know it, Billie-Blue. Back for more wild adventures with my girl.*

62

But it was three years since he'd disappeared down that stairwell. Two years and nine months since she'd been allowed to visit him in prison. Eleven months since his last letter. How many days was that? Billie had a new crack in her heart for every single one of them.

Dad must be out any day now – maybe he was out already, whatever Mam said. Billie had counted off the days of his sentence – the two thirds that he would serve *as long as he behaved himself.* And he would have done. He wouldn't want to be in that place a second longer than he had to. Couldn't bear it. Couldn't bear being away from his family.

Had he changed his mind about coming back to them? To Billie?

Or lied about it, like he lied to his boss about the money he stole?

Her heart-voice pushed its way through the tangle of hurt in her head: pure and clear as birdsong.

Dad would NEVER lie to Billie. Not ever.

And he would never abandon her. Whatever Mam said . . .

Pain pebbles pushed their way between her ribs and into her throat. How could she have believed that – let anger swallow her like a hungry whale?

63

She laid the binoculars on her bed. She'd keep them out now. Use them. She wrapped Dad's green scarf around her neck, swallowing hard. No scent of his skin there now in its soft fibres. She peered into the box. Nothing else. Where was Dad's book: the one on British birds? The one with the robin on the front cover. Billie was *sure* she'd put it in there. It was precious to her.

Perhaps she'd got muddled. Maybe it had got boxed up with all Dad's other things, stashed in the tiny spare room until Daniel commandeered it for his 'office'. *So you know where they are, Billie, love*, Mam had said. *Any time you want them: there they'll be.*

But Billie *hadn't* wanted them, had she? Not until now. She'd wanted them out of sight. Like Dad was. As if not seeing them, not touching them might help heal her heart. Her jaw tightened. But now, because of Daniel, they'd been banished to the cold, grimy garage, which made Billie feel guilty all over again.

Dad *would* come home soon. She was sure of it. He *had* to. And how would he feel when he found out that she hadn't kept his things safe for him? Hadn't kept them close. She'd been hurt and angry and she'd let him down. But so had Mam. She was still married to him. That didn't change just because Dad had committed a crime, even though Mam said *something like that changes everything* . . .

Familiar feelings jostled for space in Billie's head, tangled and twisted together like the vines and spiky branches in Tanglewood. However often she tried, she couldn't see her way through them. What was Mam *doing*, being with Daniel, deciding to move him in like Dad didn't exist? Now, when it was time for Dad to come home? How could she do that to him? To *Billie*?

Fury swelled in her chest. Mam was the one to blame, the one to be angry with. Billie felt the sting of her nails, sharp inside her balled-up fists . . .

But then, Daniel had moved into Mam's head too, hadn't he? He'd stolen the space where Mam was Mam, just like he stole the warmth from rooms and the words from Billie's mouth.

Daniel had wanted to move in. And what Daniel wants, Daniel gets.

How could she blame Mam when Mam wasn't Mam any more?

Billie felt lost in the tangle of it all. The only thing she knew for sure was that she needed Dad.

A muffled cry came from the hat-nest – rasping, dry. More like a croak than the call of a bird. Billie jumped. Water. The poor bird must need water.

She pulled herself away from her impossible thought-maze; away from the box with its pieces of Dad – pieces of *her*. She pulled her thick green jumper from her drawer and used it to line the box. She lowered the hat-nest into one corner and circled the jumper around it, like it was cradled in the arms of a summer-green tree. One black bead eye watched her as she closed the cardboard flaps, leaving a small air space between them.

'You'll be safe like that,' she whispered through the crack. 'But don't worry. I'll be back in a minute.'

She crept to the bathroom, removed her toothbrush from its plastic mug and filled the cup with water. Would the bird drink from that? She doubted it. It smelled of mint toothpaste. What could she use? She rooted around among bottles, tubs and packets of painkillers – careful not to move Daniel's shaving things. Even though they had no right to be there. A small, plastic syringe rolled towards her. Like the one Mam used to deliver pink stringy medicine into her clamped-shut mouth when she was a baby – too tiny to understand that this would help her. Maybe that could work for the bird. She rinsed it under the tap, drew water into it from the plastic cup and slid it up under the sleeve of her sweatshirt.

The bird was having none of it. It startled as Billie's hand loomed above it with the syringe; froze again. Crystal beads of water landed on its head, hung from its closed beak for a moment, ran down its black feathers like rain on a night-time window.

'Please, Bird,' Billie whispered. 'You have to.'

It was no good. Was the bird too weak even to drink? Or was she – the purple giant – the problem? She slid her coat from her shoulders, hoped the conker-brown of her sweatshirt would be less of a threat.

She squirted water into the shallow lid of her pencil tin and wedged it among the green folds of her jumper, close to the bird. As she moved away, a door slammed. Bathroom or kitchen? Billie couldn't tell. Either way, it was the kind of slam that Billie got into trouble for.

A Daniel door-slam.

The boom of his full-stop voice. 'Billie. Lunch.'

She had to go.

She tucked the bird box under her bed. 'Back as soon as I can, Bird,' she whispered into the dusty darkness. She pulled the edge of the duvet down low, tucked the cup and syringe behind her curtains.

'Billie? Come on, love.' Mam, this time, an edge of worry in her voice. Daniel did *not* like being ignored . . .

Billie took off her shoes, kicked one of them across the floor. It should be Daniel locked away in that starless prison, not her dad. Why couldn't he just disappear?

EIGHT

Daniel was silent for most of the meal, shovelling shepherd's pie into his mouth without looking up except to raise an eyebrow at Billie when her knife scrape-screeched against her plate. The air felt heavy and hot, even though Billie's feet were freezing under the table.

Mam had her Daniel smile painted on her face. It was like she kept it in a drawer or something and got it out whenever he was around just to please him. It didn't make her eyes into small, shiny stars like the smiles she wore when she first met him. Before he started staying over and unpacking his real storm-self bit by bit with his boxes of belongings.

'Daniel's got the rest of the weekend off, Billie,' Mam said, her drawer-smile pinned in place. 'He's got a long-haul drive next week, so they've said he can take a break; rest up before he goes. So . . .' She paused, looked at Daniel, pulled her smile wider. 'I thought we could do something together tomorrow – as a family. Go somewhere. A lovely winter walk, maybe.' She pointed towards the window, towards the heavy sky. 'Looks like it might snow.' The smile crept into her eyes for the first time, made small crinkles at the corners. '*And* Billie, they've got some sledges in at the garage Co-op. Perhaps we could –'

'Waste of money.' Daniel threw down his knife and fork, sat back in his chair. 'Plastic rubbish.' He drained his cup of tea, pushed it in Mam's direction. 'Anyway, it's raining tomorrow. So no snow, thank God. I don't want to be driving in that stuff next week.'

The smile dropped from Mam's face. She reached for Daniel's cup, jumped up and flipped the switch of the kettle. When she turned round, the smile was back.

'Well, then, we could watch a film together or something,' she said, her eyes darting between Daniel and Billie. 'What d'you think?'

Billie put down her knife and fork, moved them neatly together before Daniel could say anything about table manners. But no way was she spending 'family-time' with *him*. Even for a minute. She was only here at all because of the bird. As soon as she could, she'd be back on her way to find Dad.

'Thanks, Mam,' she said. 'But I said I'd meet a friend tomorrow. Maybe go to her house.'

Daniel poured extra milk into his second cup of tea, which wasn't quite the right shade of brown, judging by his straight-line mouth. 'I thought you didn't have any friends round here,' he said. 'Thought you were a proper "Billie-no-Mates",' he added, grinning now.

Billie glanced at Mam, who smiled again, reached across and brushed Billie's curls from her forehead.

'Course she has friends,' Mam said. 'It just takes a bit of time, that's all, when you move somewhere new.' She stirred sugar into her own mug of tea and clutched it between her hands.

Daniel yawned and stretched his legs out under the table. 'Never had that problem myself,' he said. He fixed Billie with his ice-grey eyes. 'Got moved around every year when I was a boy. Whether I liked it or not. Just had to get on with it. Kids were queuing up to be my mate everywhere I went.'

Billie stood up, took her plate to the drainer, and started to fill the sink with hot water. She squeezed the bottle of detergent harder than needed, sending a fierce green jet into the bowl. Bubbles swirled and surged under the tap. She felt them inside her stomach too. Inside her head, fizzing and filling it too full. Why would anyone want to be Daniel's friend? She bit down on the words pushing

71

their way up through her throat. This was one of *those* Daniel days. Not a day to answer back. Not a day to say anything at all, or someone – most likely Mam but maybe Billie too – would bear the brunt of a Daniel-storm unleashed. A storm-voice that shook the windows and stung like hailstones. Ice-sliver whispers that sliced at your heart and made you to blame. Thunder and lightning fists that split the air and sometimes struck a person, even though Daniel *never meant that to happen*.

You didn't get to choose which kind of storm. It was pot-luck.

Mam joined Billie at the sink. Billie felt her hand warm on her back. Comfort, or storm-warning. Both, probably. But she shifted away from it, spun round, as this time, some words escaped, anyway.

'My friend's called Nell, if you must know,' she said, staring hard at Daniel, then at Mam, then at the floor. 'She lives in York Court and I'm going there for tea tomorrow. So you two can have a cosy film afternoon all to yourselves.' She turned back to the sink and swiped the used cutlery into the soapy water, sent a tiny escapee bubble to hang in the still air along with her words.

'You don't speak to your mam like that,' Danny said after way too long. 'And seeing as you're all friendly with this Nell, you can stop complaining about the move, can't you? Kids these days.' He shook his head. 'You think everything should revolve around you!'

Billie's ears grew hot. Who did he think he was? She gritted her teeth, scrubbed at a fork; threw it on to the drainer, pretended to fish in the water for more. She imagined his face, growing redder by the second. The twitch of his right cheek. First sign of the storm – like the metallic scent on the wind just before rain. Had it started? You had to watch for that. She didn't dare check.

Mam reached for a clean plate, began wiping it dry with a tea towel. Her hands moved scared-slow, round and round. She watched them. Billie watched them. The air had left the room.

She should have kept quiet. She should apologise.

And she should turn round. Daniel didn't like people's backs.

She didn't turn back.

Neither did Mam.

Billie heard Daniel's silent stare at her mam; heard his heavy sigh and the exasperated scream of his chair, the slap of his stupid slippers on the floor as he stomped from the room and down the hall to the bathroom. She waited for the click of the lock, the hiss of the shower. She turned round.

The kitchen door stood wide open, like an unfinished argument. Billie hoped Mam wouldn't have to finish it when Daniel got back from the pub. Daniel storms didn't blow over; blow away. They just gathered power, blew back in when you least expected it. She chewed at her lip and brushed what might have been bubbles from her cheek.

Mam cleared her throat, brushed invisible crumbs from the worktop into the palm of her hand. 'So, sweetheart,' she said. Her smile was back, but her voice sounded thin, like some of it was trapped somewhere inside her. 'You've made a new friend. That's lovely. Is she in your class? You could ask her round for tea next weekend. How about that?'

Billie grabbed a pan from the bench, thrust it into the water. She hated lying to Mam. Hated that Daniel was angry with her now. But it was Mam's own fault. Everything was. Mam was the one who'd made Billie leave their home – made her leave Dad's garden. Their bird trees. Their starlit skies. Mam was the one who'd made her move to a school where everyone sniggered at her red hair and kept saying her dad was a 'skanky thief'.

Liars. She hated them.

Most of all, she hated Daniel. And right now, even though she was worried for her, she hated Mam too. Mam was the one who'd brought Daniel into their family and behaved like everything was better now.

That was the biggest lie of all.

Billie dried her hands, threw the towel on the floor, and pushed past Mam towards the door. She glanced into the hall. Could Daniel still hear anything? She wasn't sure. She pulled the kitchen door closed and pressed her back against it.

'I can't have *anyone* round for tea with him here,' she hissed. 'I can't even go to Nell's for tea tomorrow like she asked me. I made that up. There's no point in making any friends. *You* haven't got any, have you? Not any more. Not since Daniel. Daniel doesn't let you.' She turned away to hide her trembling chin and stalked out of the kitchen, her legs stiff as stone.

She held her breath, tried to settle the thump-thud of her heart. What had she done? She should never have answered back to Daniel. His anger would hang in the air like a storm cloud, heavy and waiting to burst. There'd be more sharp-glass silences and tiptoe-tense hours until it did. Billie thought of the blue-flower bruises on Mam's wrist. She shivered.

Back in her room, her legs didn't want to hold her up any more. They trembled under her weight like the twig legs of the bird underneath her bed. She took a few deep breaths, knelt, and peered underneath, her tangled hair brushing the floor. How was the bird doing now? She hoped it wasn't feeling even more afraid than before; that it couldn't sense the new Daniel-danger it faced.

'Hello, Bird,' she whispered. 'Don't worry. I won't let him find you.' She drew the box gently towards her, keeping the draped edge of the duvet over half of it so that the bird felt partly hidden, like when it limped away to huddle behind the play park tree. It was hunched, smaller somehow. But it was still, at least, eyes closed, no longer shivering. It *might* have been asleep, Billie wasn't sure. There were clear beads of water on its green wool bed, dark damp specks on the cardboard sides of the box. Perhaps it had taken a drink then. She should probably leave it alone for now; try later with food.

Maybe she should try to sleep too. Maybe by the time she woke, Daniel would have left for the pub. She could only hope this was one of those times when beer and beery mates would smooth out his sharp edges; make him forget. But what were the chances of that? He might even come storming into her room right now with his jabbing, gripping, fingers that left blue prints on Mam's wrist *because he'd had a stinker of a day, and Mam winding him up was the last straw, but it would never happen again, and that was a promise.* He had cried. Mam had cried. Billie's tears stayed frozen behind her eyes.

It *would* happen again. She knew it would.

She just didn't know what to do about it.

She had stayed awake all night, listening for another storm, wondering how to prevent one. She had fallen asleep in class the next day. Ms Rahman had looked at her with questions in her eyes and wrinkles on her brow since that day. Sometimes, she asked her questions. Billie didn't give any answers. She daren't.

If she told the truth, the school would send someone to the flat – a social-worker or something. Make Daniel angrier than ever. Billie might be taken into Care; be made to live with strangers far from her home like Aaron Campbell in her class: far away, where Dad might not be able to find her ever again. She wasn't risking any of that.

But she could still see the press of those fingers; still see the red veins in Daniel's eyes as his face loomed close to Mam's. The fear in Mam's face. Panic rose, fluttered in her chest like frantic wings. Her head felt tight and hot.

She listened, heard the thump-thud of Daniel's music from the bedroom.

Come on, Billie. Breathe. He was getting ready for his precious night out with the lads. That was all he cared about right now. He'd be gone soon . . .

Billie shuffled forward, eased the bird box back out of sight – just in case. She put Dad's binoculars under her pillow and hid the rest of his belongings inside a spare pillowcase, at the back of her wardrobe. She lay back on the bed, one hand curled around the binoculars and closed her eyes. But pictures kept scudding across the back of her eyelids: a flicker-book she didn't want to read. Daniel's changeling face: the wide smile that could disappear in an instant, like the wind had taken it; the flat-line mouth and thunder brow that blew in to replace it for no reason at all. The twitching cheek and tight-ball fists: red-light warnings of those building storms. Those heavy, gripping fingers.

She pulled the binoculars on to her chest; gripped them tightly. Why, *why* he had stopped writing? Why wasn't he out of prison yet, here with Billie? Here to send Daniel packing and make her and Mam safe?

And if he *was* out already, why hadn't he come?

Dad's field-green eyes swam into focus behind Billie's

eyelids: soft and out of place against the harsh white lights and dirty yellow walls of the prison visiting room. His usually busy, kind hands, now folded and still on the scratched red table. His untouched plastic cup of tea. His smile that pretended to be fine.

She heard the clink and rattle of chain and key; the boom of the guard's voice calling time. The clang of the goodbye doors between them. Since then – for *two years and nine months* – not a single prison visiting order with Billie and Mam's names spider-scrawled across the page. No more visits. Just a few thin, butterfly-blue letters escaping the prison walls to land on their morning mat. And even those had stopped last Christmas. *Could* Dad have forgotten them? Was he moving on without them, like Daniel said? Like *Mam* said.

No. Daniel didn't know anything. And Mam was just trying to make herself feel better about being with him when she was still married to Dad.

Perhaps Dad was sick. Mam believed that they'd get told if he was, but she wouldn't ring the prison to check, not even to make Billie feel better. Since she met Daniel, it was like she just wanted to block Dad out completely. Rub him out of Billie's mind just like she'd done in her own.

What if, without his wind and stars world, without his

family, Dad had just given up? Shut down, like the little rabbit imprisoned by the crows. *Wild things belong to the wild, Billie-Blue. They don't do well anywhere else. Best leave them be. Leave them free*

An iron bar of pain pressed down on Billie's chest, made it hard to breathe. She turned on her stomach, pressed her face into the bed, and covered her ears with her hands. The duvet grew damp against her cheeks.

A knock at the bedroom door. Mam's face peered into the room, plaster-pale in the closed curtain gloom.

'Billie? You OK, sweetheart?'

Billie's heartbeat leaped into her ears. Bird. In its box. Could Mam see it? Had she hidden it properly?

She let one arm drop over the side of the bed; felt only the drape of the duvet; no scratch of the cardboard box. Good. *But please keep still, Bird*, Billie pleaded in her head. *Please don't make a sound . . .*

The mattress dipped beside Billie. Mam's fingers were gentle in her hair. Billie moved away from them.

'Where's Daniel?' Billie muttered into the wet, cold duvet. 'Has he gone yet?'

Mam nodded. 'To the pub. Just for a bit.'

It would *not* be 'for a bit'. He'd be there until closing time; would arrive home after midnight, with banging doors, staggering feet and loud words that fell over themselves in the dark.

Billie turned and lifted herself to rest on one elbow. She looked up at Mam. The blue flower bruise on her wrist was fading now. But Mam couldn't have forgotten; couldn't believe her own story about the edge of a closing door and *you know me; never watch what I'm doing* . . .

'Don't wait up for him this time, Mam,' she said. 'Don't. He's already in a bad mood and he hadn't even had his beers yet . . .'

Mam sighed; ran a finger along Billie's cheek.

'He didn't mean anything at lunchtime, love. He just, you know, doesn't always think. He's not used to . . . family life. Children.' Her mouth twitched, wobbled. Like she might cry too. Instead, she smiled – a quick, darting smile that was gone almost as soon as it arrived. 'He'll get better at it.' She stroked Billie's arm. 'He wants to. And he's promised to go easy tonight – just a couple of drinks, and not too late home.'

Billie stared at her. Why did she believe a word Daniel said, after everything? Why did she always make excuses for him? Why couldn't she just *see*?

'You won't though, will you? Wait up for him? You don't

have to just because he says so. He can make his own stupid late snack.'

'It's fine, Billie. Really. I don't mind, anyway.'

'He shouldn't do it, though,' Billie said, through clenched teeth. She shifted away from Mam's touch. 'He shouldn't order you about, and he shouldn't drink so much and shout and – do that.' She nodded at Mam's wrist, pulled at her hair and squinted at Mam through red tangles. 'Dad never did.'

'He needs his down-time, Billie. Needs to unwind. He works hard. For us.'

'So do you,' Billie said. 'So did Dad.' Billie swallowed past the lump in her throat, looked away from her mam's face, the new shadows under her eyes.

Mam's hand drifted to her wrist, encircled it. 'That was an accident, Billie. A – mistake. It won't happen again.'

Billie glared at her. *A mistake*? He *hurt* you, Mam. On purpose. And you forgive him, just like that. Make excuses for him. What about Dad then? How come you don't forgive *him*? How come you don't even like saying his name any more? His mistake wasn't anything as bad and he's my *dad* and you won't even talk about him!'

Mam stared past Billie, like part of her had left the room already. She shook her head, sighed. Billie grabbed her hands, clasped them between her own. She'd give this one last try . . .

'Dad's coming out soon, Mam. Maybe he's already out. We can be a family again. We could move to a new place. Away from here. Away from Daniel. Please, ring the prison again. Or let's just go there. Let's find out where he is and make sure he's OK; tell him we're waiting for him.'

Mam glanced at the ceiling, at her feet, like she was searching for words there.

'No, love,' she said, soft as a sigh. 'Your dad made his choice, *he* left *us*. I want to move on, to make a go of things with Daniel. We just need time, that's all. And like I've said, I'm sure someone from the prison would have been in touch if anything's changed, or if he was out already.' She stood up and straightened Billie's duvet, smoothed it with her hands. 'Unless . . . unless Dad doesn't want them to for some reason, I suppose.'

Billie stared at her. 'What do you mean?' she whispered, her throat dry.

Mam shook her head. 'Honestly, Billie, I don't know. But we'll see him soon enough, I'm sure. If we don't, well, that tells us all we need to know, doesn't it?'

Billie sat up, poker-straight, looked Mam in the eye. 'How can you say that? You *know* Dad wouldn't just abandon us. You *do*. He'll *be* here. And then he'll find out what *you've* done, how you've swapped him for Daniel and made everything horrible and dangerous and unhappy. He won't let him stay; you'll see. Dad loves us. He does.'

Mam stroked Billie's hand; sighed a soft sigh.

'I know this is hard, Billie, love. I do. And I know how much you love your dad. But things have changed between Dad and me, and there's no good pretending they haven't. I'm with Daniel now. And we want to make this work. Daniel thinks a lot of you, you know, in his own way. So, yes, your dad and I need to talk, and we will – when he's out of prison and we can have a proper conversation. If he gets in touch again. And we'll talk about *you*, Billie. When the time is right, that will happen, I promise.' She fiddled with a loose thread on the duvet, wound it around one finger. A small hole opened in the fabric.

'Look at this old thing,' Mam said. 'We must get you a new one . . .'

'I don't need a new one,' Billie said. She jumped to her feet without having known she was going to. 'I just need Dad. Back here where he belongs. And NO Daniel. *Please*, please, Mam.'

Mam stood up, brushed her hands over the duvet, straightened it so that it hung evenly across the bed.

'I don't know what to say to you any more, love, I really don't.' She crossed to Billie's clothes basket, pulled out her school sweatshirts and trousers, bundled them in her arms. 'I'll explain things to your dad, *when I* see him. When I *know* he's going to be responsible and wants to be involved with you still. We'll make it work so that you have time together. Just leave it to me now, OK? This is grown-up business. There's a lot you're too young to understand.'

Angry words pushed at Billie's throat. This was *her dad* they were talking about. Mam might want to throw him away like an old sock, but she couldn't expect Billie to. It was *Mam* that didn't understand anything. And she wasn't even behaving like a grown-up herself. Not a proper one. A proper grown-up – a proper *mam* would have kept Billie safe from people like Daniel.

Billie opened her mouth to speak. Snapped it shut.

Mam was bending down, reaching for something under the edge of the chest of drawers. Was the bird box visible?

Billie sat down on the bed again, shuffled her legs along the edge to shield the spot where she'd put the box. Mam stood up, one fluffy sock in her hand.

'Been there a while, this one,' she said, painting her new smile back into place. Changing the subject. 'Are you hungry? How about we get a sandwich? Maybe watch a film. Just the two of us, eh? There might be some popcorn in the cupboard.'

Billie felt for the box with her heels, inched it further under the bed. She drew in a jagged breath, tried to steady her angry heartbeat. Best get Mam out of the room as quickly as possible, she thought. Their conversation was pointless, anyway. She couldn't rely on Mam to sort anything. She didn't care about Dad any more. Billie would sort things herself just as soon as Bird was safe.

It'd only be a couple of days, surely. Then she'd be able to get back to her plan. Back to finding Dad. She couldn't leave it any longer. If he left before she got to the prison, she wasn't sure anyone would tell her where he'd gone. She *couldn't* miss him.

For now, she just needed to let the bird rest. To keep it hidden. To keep the peace and not give Mam – or Daniel – a reason to suspect anything at all.

'OK then,' she muttered. 'Suppose a film would be nice . . .'

'Right. Lovely.' Mam scurried from the room, leaving the air stiff with lost words and unanswered questions. But at least she hadn't discovered the bird. It was safe. For now.

NINE

Billie lay in bed listening for the fumble of a key in the front door, the stumble of Saturday footsteps in the hall. So far, the night was unusually still and quiet. Just muffled TV voices from next door through the thin walls and, once, the unearthly scream of a cat. There was a metallic scent on the air that squeezed through the cracked pane above Billie's head. Rain was coming. She had known it was on its way, had spotted the tell-tale raggedy clouds overhead in the last of the daylight. More sky writing if you bothered to read it. And Billie did. Especially now she needed to keep focused on her plan to run away. Needed to watch for the weather stories, pick the best day to set out, and prepare as best she could for whatever was to come on her journey.

The bird was quiet. It had ignored the breadcrumb supper Billie had offered it. She had sprinkled the crumbs in the box, along with a sliver of bacon rind retrieved from the kitchen bin. She had no idea whether it was old enough to manage solid food – or whether 'human' food might do more harm than good. But it was all she could find for now. For all she knew, the little thing might die of starvation – or food poisoning, before sunrise. She didn't want to sleep while it did.

Anyway, however angry she was with Mam, she needed to make sure she was OK.

And she hadn't heard her come to bed yet.

Billie stretched out, hands behind her head, and watched the chase of moon shadows across the ceiling, the occasional spin of night-time headlights around the walls.

The room grew darker and darker. The TV voices grew silent. Mam's footsteps sounded softly in the hall on the way to her room and the spatter of the first raindrops on the window lulled Billie into unexpected sleep.

Billie opened her eyes, her head still sleep-swimmy, not properly awake. It was daylight – well, no longer night-time dark. The blue face of her alarm clock read 6.15 a.m. But she hadn't heard Daniel. No Saturday night crashing around.

What did that mean? Had Daniel stayed out? She

hoped so. Hoped he would stay out forever.

Should she tiptoe to Mam's room, make sure she was all right?

No. Daniel would go ballistic if he *was* there. Best just wait. Billie wasn't supposed to disturb anyone until 9 a.m. on a Sunday. Another of Daniel's stupid rules.

She sighed, shuffled to the far edge of her bed, away from the damp air leaking in through the cracked window.

The she remembered.

The bird.

Her heart thudded. Once. Twice.

She listened; strained her ears like a night-time owl. Just the spit-spot of rain on the window and her blood swooshing in her ears like wild wind through the Tanglewood trees.

Was it still alive? If it was, it must be able to hear that too.

The room narrowed to the space between Billie and the box under her bed.

She had to know.

She wriggled out of the covers; leaned over the side of the bed, head dangling down in the freezing air. Her breath drifted like smoke over water. She peered through her hair into the darkness at the pale sides of the box. She moved one arm snake-slow towards it, tapped with a fingernail against the side. Waited.

Nothing.

No flutter of feathers. Not even a scratch of scaly claw.

It was dead. She'd known it would be.

She should have listened to Dad. Let the little thing be back there at the play park. She had failed the bird and it was gone. Just like Dad.

The cold crept inside her chest, settled right in the middle. Her heart ached and burned, like it was being turned to ice.

Then it came. A soft scuffle-scrape. Claws on cardboard. Must be.

Billie wriggled down on to her stomach, reached for the box. She inched her hand towards the lid, held her breath. She lifted one of the flaps, careful-slow; peered down into the red knitted nest.

No bird.

She lifted a second flap, searched among the folds of her green sweater.

Nothing.

The bird had gone.

Billie pushed herself up to kneel on the bed and scanned the room, fingers crossed behind her back that she would not spot it stiff and lifeless on the floor. The ice in her chest spread to her throat, made it hard to breathe.

A small movement on the chest of drawers.

'There you are,' Billie said, her voice cracked; strange. 'Thank goodness.' Her struggling breath rushed out; brought with it a sob she didn't know was coming. The bird was alive – and apparently feeling much better. She slid from the bed and crawled across the carpet, afraid to stand in case her size spooked it. 'So you *can* fly?'

The bird blinked and stared at Billie from behind her one-eared childhood teddy and a pile of school workbooks. Today, its eyes burned beetle-bright; spoke to Billie of wildness and wide skies. Her heart lifted a little.

The bird opened its beak, made its strange rasping cry. More like frog-speak than bird language, Billie thought. The beak opened again, showing a scarlet throat. No sound this time. It was asking for food – surely. Or a drink. Both, probably.

'OK, Bird,' Billie whispered. 'Wait a minute. I'll get you something.'

The bird closed its eyes, started trembling again – maybe from weakness, or maybe Billie's voice – Billie *moving* was still too much for it. But if she could get it to take food and water from her this time, perhaps it might come to trust her more; not be quite so scared. Scared was horrible. Scared needed to stop.

But what could she feed it *with*?

She shuffled back towards the bird box. The bacon rind was still there, shrivelled and coated in crumbs. Ravens ate meat, she knew – but perhaps bacon was too salty? Too tough?

'Don't blame you, Bird,' Billie said. 'I don't like it either. We've got to do better than that.'

She thought of the birds in Tanglewood, of sitting cat-quiet like Dad had taught her, watching them forage and feed and live their bird lives. The blackbirds and spotted thrush poking around for worms and tiny insects among the tapestry of moss, curled leaves and burnished-brown conkers. The darting finches and quick sparrows snatching at autumn berries in the bushes. And best of all, the ravens, surveying the scene from their high-wire evergreen perches like ancient bird-gods, or sailing in the air above the treetops, like small planes on the air currents, carrying their stories on their wings.

That was it. She would take the bird back to the wood again. Maybe this time, having rested a bit, it *would* fly off and feed itself anyway. If not, she could do some foraging of her own on its behalf. The only trouble was, Mam wouldn't want her going out in the rain. Would it stop by the morning? The proper morning, that was.

She edged her way to the bed and knelt up at the window. She lifted a corner of the curtain, rubbed at the glass, and peered outside. Nothing much to see at this early hour. Just the hard edges of neighbouring tower blocks grey against the black November sky; the pavement shiny under the sickly street lamp closest to the block. It had rained hard overnight, washed away yesterday's ice-white world. She had read the sky writing correctly. The rain-soaked, thawed woodland floor would make it easy for foraging birds to find the scurrying insects there, under the sodden leaves; easier to pull up worms that wriggled in the softened earth. Definitely a good time to tempt the young raven to fend for itself.

The rain was still falling but it was a light drizzle now, drifting slowly down past the window. Hopefully, it was almost done, and Mam would only insist she wore her wellies and raincoat. Although if Daniel *was* back, and sleeping off his night-out headache, she would probably be relieved to have Billie out of the way. And that suited Billie fine too. Even if it was still pouring down.

'Breakfast in Tanglewood for you then, Bird,' Billie said. 'Just as soon as it's properly light. OK?'

The bird cocked its head to one side, kept on staring as Billie dressed in yesterday's clothes, slowly so as not to startle it. All she had to do now was persuade it back into its box when she went downstairs for breakfast. It couldn't stay where it was. Not with Daniel anywhere around.

The bird was having none of it. Each time Billie lowered it into the green sweater nest and tried to close the cardboard flaps over its head, it squawked in protest – and at a volume that could surely be heard from outside the room. Each time she tried to settle it with whispered words it lifted its wings and fluttered back to hide behind its teddy bear accomplice.

'OK,' Billie said. 'You can stay there. But just please, please be quiet.'

TEN

'Slow down, Billie,' Mam said. 'You'll give yourself indigestion. And how about some porridge as well? Toast won't keep you going for very long.'

'Sorry,' Billie sputtered, through a huge mouthful of toast. 'No, thanks. Full up.'

But when Mam turned to scoop porridge into her bowl, she crammed an even larger piece into her mouth; stuffed another into her pocket. She was starving, but she needed to be super quick. Daniel hadn't come home yet: he'd stayed over at his mate's house, Mam said. He would be back some time – *any* time – this morning though, and Billie had to smuggle the bird out of the flat before that happened. Given his new noisy behaviour, it would be tricky enough to get him past Mam, let alone eagle-eyed Daniel.

'What's your rush, Billie?' Mam said. 'Can't you wait for Daniel? I think he might want to . . . you know . . . smooth things over after yesterday. Apologise. He said something about a cinema trip . . .'

Billie shook her head, swallowed the last of her toast. Was Mam for real? Cinema trips with pretend smiles and popcorn; pizza and ice cream, afterwards – *as much as she wanted* – they were a thing of the past. A Daniel-Before-He-Moved-In-Pretending-To-Be-Nice thing that had slipped further and further away with every night Daniel spent at the flat, even though Mam refused to see it. Billie didn't fall for it any more. And Live-In-Daniel didn't do apologies. Or if he did, he didn't mean them.

'I'm meeting Nell, remember?' she said, avoiding Mam's eyes. 'Well, not meeting her exactly, just we might see one another in the play park. And I've to get going before it rains again.' She gulped down her glass of milk, jumped up and placed it in the sink. 'Nell's nan won't let her out if it's too wet,' she added, for extra credibility.

'Quite right,' Mam said. 'I want you back too, if it gets heavy. And before you're soaked through, not after, mind. And wear your –'

'Mac and wellies. I know. I will,' Billie said. 'And look,' she added, reaching down a jar of peanut butter from the cupboard. 'I'm making sandwiches to take, OK?'

Mam sighed. 'Well, yes, good. But Billie ... You can't ... I don't want you . . . staying out all day. You and Daniel, you just need to spend more time together, get to know each other.'

Billie pressed down the top of her sandwich with rather too much force, creating a buttery explosion on her plate. She managed a small nod. Even that was a lie. She'd tried to like Daniel. She had. Even though she'd hated him on sight just because he wasn't Dad. She'd tried because for a while, Daniel had eased the worry lines from Mam's face, quietened her night time tears.

But there wasn't time for an argument now. She needed to escape.

The bird hopped away from Billie's hands when she tried to catch it. It fluttered to the floor, then up on to her bedside table. She crawled after it, sat with her back to it, knees on her chin. What should she try now? She could throw her pyjama jacket over it, she supposed, trap it like in a net. But that would be terrifying for it. Best to ignore it for a bit, she decided; get all ready to leave and then try again.

As she pushed her arms into the flapping sleeves of her navy raincoat, the bird began a madcap dance of panicked wing beats, jumps and flutters; almost skidded over the edge of the cupboard at the clonk of the belt buckle that swung out of reach behind her.

'You don't like this coat either, do you? I'm taking it off, bird. See?' Billie eased the coat from her shoulders, scrunched it into a ball.

But the bird lifted into the air, hurled itself at a small, bright gap between the curtains.

'No, don't! You'll hurt yourself.' Billie bent and shoved the raincoat out of sight.

'It's gone. Look. It's OK.'

The bird dropped on to Billie's bed, eyes wilder than ever.

'Sorry, Bird,' Billie said. 'I know this isn't your world, and it's all so scary. But I'm trying to help, I really am. You need food, so we've *got* to go out.' She bit her lip, stemmed the wobble there. If only he could understand.

The bird shook itself and hunkered down, eyelids heavy now.

'Worn yourself out, haven't you?' Billie whispered.

She slipped down from the bed and moved snake-slow towards her wardrobe. She slid inside and retrieved her purple coat from its depths. She might be a purple monster in this, but at least she would be a familiar one. Worth a try.

It worked. This time the bird made no attempt to escape her hands, allowed her to cradle its cloud-body and zip it back safely against her chest. Billie picked up the navy gabardine terror, drew it around her shoulders and slung her backpack on top to hold it in place. The raincoat floated around her arms like wings as she walked down the stairway from the flats, trying to shield the bird from the noisy clump of her wellies. Once outside, she scrunched it into a ball and stuffed it inside her backpack, where it could do no more harm.

Her spirits lifted and fell, lifted and fell, as she strode towards Tanglewood. It was good to be away from the flat, away from Daniel again. But would Mam be OK? Should Billie have hung around, waited to see what kind of mood Daniel was in? Then again, the sooner this little bird was back where it belonged and thriving, the better for the bird and for Billie. Because then she could go and find Dad. He would help her, and he would know how to help Mam.

Billie's mood settled as she pushed her way under the first glistening fronds and branches of the wet wood. She stood still, listened to the patter of rain on the evergreen leaf canopy. She watched the slow roll of water-diamonds from leaf and branch, followed their steady-soft drip on to the thick forest floor; smiled as one landed, ice-cold, in her hair and another trickled down her nose. Tanglewood in the rain. Billie loved it. It was like the world was being washed clean and fresh and new. If only. She drew in deep breaths, felt the freshness inside herself . . . just for a moment.

The rich scent of soaked earth rose in her nostrils, took her back to the garden at Lambert Drive – to standing with Dad under the dripping fir in the fresh-soaked morning air: *Smell that, Billie-Blue? The smell of life, that's what that is. They can't bottle that for your mam's dressing table. There's nothing like it. And it's totally free.*

Billie thought of the prison: of the single strip of grass outside the visiting room, parched and dry, rubbed away by hundreds of feet hurrying across it to snatch a few minutes with their father, brother, son. The spiked wire fence that kept life *out*. Billie had told Dad about Tanglewood in a letter, pictured the light in his eyes as he imagined it. He'd received the letter, Billie was sure. She'd copied the address exactly from the last letter he sent to her and Mam. She'd posted it herself too. But Dad had never replied. Billie had begged Mam to check with the prison that it had been received. She did. And *they* did. *They couldn't tell her any more at the time*, Mam said.

Doubt still twisted inside Billie, curled around her intestines, sharp and cruel and spiky like the prison wire. What if the missing letters *did* mean Dad no longer wanted to come home? What if she found her way to the prison and, after all, he didn't want to know? Didn't want *her* any more? She sighed, pushing the clean, fresh air back out to float away among the trees. Her heart ached underneath the bird, heavy with hurt. Heavy with guilt for doubting Dad, even for a moment. The bird squirmed, as if the heaviness was inside him too.

The rain footsteps grew louder; heavier and faster, pushed through the trees, pelted the front of her coat. She shook droplets from the ends of her hair, tried to push away the worry. Soon enough, she'd have some answers. Right now, she should get going; search for somewhere more sheltered to release the bird so it could search for food.

She arrived at yesterday's clearing without ever having decided to go there again, as if the wood had spoken, decided for her, and drawn her to the place. She crouched under the tree-skirted entrance; rain running down her neck now. The wooden swing was still; empty. Its owner would never be out in this weather. She and the bird were alone, for now. And the saturated leaf-carpet here must be crawling with worms and other bird treats. She should try letting her passenger go, find the driest place she could to keep an eye on it.

The bird wriggled and scratched at Billie's clothes as if in agreement. It hopped to the floor as soon as she undid her coat. It looked around, head cocking from side to side, listened for the tell-tale rustle of breakfast among the wet leaves and moss.

Good. Its parents had taught it that, at least. Hopefully, it knew what to do next and would eat something, back here in its natural habitat.

Once it had moved away a little, Billie crept forward to explore the clearing for a hideout, lifting her boots slowly so as not to disturb the hungry bird or its food supply. She pushed away the thought of the unsuspecting creatures about to be snapped between its bird jaws. Like Dad said, it was the way of things.

A sharp twig-snap broke the hushed silence of the wet wood. The bird rose in a fluster of wings, landed on the thick branch that held the swing.

Billie drew in a sharp breath. Froze. Was someone – *something* – coming?

Get a grip, she thought. *There's no one. Not in this weather. You're supposed to be reassuring the bird, not scaring it.*

'Come on, Bird,' she called. 'It's nothing. Just the wood talking.' She stared up into its ancient evergreen perch. A wistful wave rose in her chest; carried forgotten whispers between Mam and Dad. Something about a summer surprise: a tree house, a tree platform, really, in the garden at Lambert Drive. Billie had overheard; imagined herself balanced in the branches with the crows and speckled thrush, close enough to reach the stars. She had held the secret that winter, warm and tingling in her chest as she drifted into sleep. But the dream – the stars, the birds – had all disappeared along with Dad. So had the Mam that planned tree-house surprises.

The bird fluttered down, landed briefly on the swing-seat; stared at Billie for moment, then hopped to the ground. It listened again for the wriggle of worms; the shuffle of insects. Billie shook herself back into the present.

'That's right, Bird,' she whispered. 'That's the way.'

A quick, soft breeze touched Billie's damp cheek, threw droplets of rain from the evergreens overhead. The swing-seat swayed slightly; steadied again. Billie looked at the cracked wooden seat, the thick ropes reaching into the arms of the tree. Might there have been a swing too, at Lambert Drive?

She moved closer, ran her fingers along the rain-soaked rope that held it, edged forward, lowered herself on to the seat. She stretched her legs out, leaned back. The swing creaked into life, groaned as it lifted her a little, fell back. Lifted. Billie closed her eyes. Let herself drift; back and forth. Back and forth. She pushed her feet down and out; swung higher and higher. Faster and faster. Until there was nothing but the rush of the air, the rain on her face. Nothing but these moments suspended between earth and sky –

Was this how it felt to fly?

Billie opened her eyes.

The bird.

What was she thinking? Had she frightened it? She scanned the ground as she swooped across it. Nothing.

But as the swing lifted again, flew high in the air, the bird came. Rose with her. Hovered above her. Swooped low to the ground as her boots caught the earth, wingbeats stirring the leaf-carpet as her toes pushed down, propelled her upwards again with a swoosh of air. Again and again, they flew together, synchronised in an aerial dance as if there was nothing but the two of them and the trees and the wind and the rain. As if time stood still to watch them fly. Billie heard a laugh. A pure shriek of joy. She realised it had come from her and that she was smiling.

Then, suddenly, the bird swerved away.

Billie let her boots drag in the earth, forced the swing to slow.

There it was. Almost close enough to touch on a nearby branch, yellow eyes glowing like headlights in the rain. Billie snatched at the ground with her heels. The swing-seat twisted from side to side; stopped. The bird's eyes found hers. This time, there was fire in them. It leaned towards her, lifted its wings again.

Something between them was changed.

'C'mon, Bird,' Billie mouthed. She stretched her arm snake-slow towards it; didn't dare to breathe. Then, the splintering of the air; the stretch and beat of dark wings.

The brush of feathers against her cheek.

Claws, slip-sliding against the shiny sleeve of her coat.

The bird hanging, scrabbling for purchase. Then the clasp of its bony feet, tight around her arm, one long toe cold against her skin where her sleeve had ridden up her wrist.

A settling of feather and wing.

A drift of dust.

A silence.

Billie stared at the gnarled dinosaur feet clasped around

her purple sleeve. The ink-black body. The curved raptor beak. The bird had never looked wilder. More 'other.' And yet she felt it. In her heart. The closing of an ancient circle. Tower-block girl, ancient winter wood, wild raven. They were one.

A dart of excitement shot through in her chest. Somehow, in some way she didn't understand, this was *her* bird. It didn't know or care who her family were, what her dad had done or why. It just saw *her*. Billie and this wild, misunderstood raven, they were friends. They belonged together.

ELEVEN

Billie had no idea how long they sat there; eyes locked together, statue-still. When she thought of it later, it was like they had disappeared together for a time. When they returned, the rain had eased to the occasional spit-spot on her cheek. A blackbird sang overhead.

The bird shook out its feathers. A last crystal bead of rain ran down his back and fell from his half-grown tail. His eyelids slid slowly down, back up again. Clockwork eyes, Billie thought, dragging herself back from wherever she had been.

Everything felt changed.

Perhaps this wasn't the time to set the bird free, after all. Perhaps they could be together just a little longer. Just till Billie set off to find Dad.

After all, Daniel was going to be away for a bit.

After all, right now, she and the bird were each other's only friend.

'What's your name, then, Bird,' Billie whispered.

The bird titled its head. Shook out its feathers.

'I don't even know if you're a boy or a girl,' Billie said. She thought for a moment. 'I think you're a boy,' she said. 'We'll say you are, anyway. But I'll just call you "Bird", OK?'

Bird scratched his beak with one long toe, made a small cronking sound.

'I'll take that as a yes then,' Billie said. 'Bird it is.'

Her stomach growled. Bird startled.

Billie smiled. 'Lunchtime, that's all,' she said. 'For both of us.'

She remembered her sandwiches – glimpsed her backpack, abandoned well out of reach at the foot of the swing-tree. Her stomach called again. She would have to get down from the swing. She pushed spirals of damp hair from her forehead. What should she do? Lower Bird to the ground? Just stand up?

Would moving break the spell?

Bird tipped his head to one side, stared into the leaf-carpet, fluttered down at her feet. A moment later, he jabbed at the ground with his beak; stretched his neck, made small, jerky movements in his throat. A little bit of lunch, apparently.

'You did it,' Billie whispered. 'Well done, Bird.' She slipped down and reached for her backpack. 'My turn now.'

The sandwiches were distinctly damp and squashed, but they filled the hole in Billie's stomach. As she bit into her last piece, a worm surfaced and wriggled across Bird's foot. He watched it, mesmerised, let it disappear back under the leaves. Billie smiled. More learning to be done, after all. Or maybe he was just full.

She broke off the edge of her sandwich, threw it down in front of him. He stabbed it, waved it from side to side, then lobbed it into a patch of moss.

Billie laughed. 'C'mon, Bird,' she said, brushing sticky crumbs from her fingers. 'Let's find something better.'

Bird hopped between Billie's hands as they sifted through drenched leaves and moss, filling her sandwich box with fresh, wriggling bird food. She felt a stab of guilt as she pressed the lid firmly closed, ending their woodland freedom with a snap. But Bird needed to eat. How long would this food supply last?

Uncertainty squirmed in Billie's stomach.

She watched him sift among moss at the base of the oak, then hop easily on to a low branch, clearly eating some morsel he had found for himself. He looked . . . at home. Healthy, now. A bubble burst in her chest. Those moments on the swing – what had she been thinking? She glanced at the squirm and press of life under the plastic lid of her sandwich box. Thought of the box-nest under her bed. Of Dad in his concrete prison. Of her own boxy bedroom in the brick tower-block flat. Of walls that pressed closer in the night, made it hard to breathe. Now that Bird seemed well, was it fair to keep him from freedom, from fresh air, even for a while?

And she had school tomorrow. He'd be locked away all day. Imprisoned. Alone. Her heart twisted. This *wasn't* her bird. *Couldn't* be. She had to help him to be himself: wild raven. Wild and free. And that meant walking away, didn't it? Right now, before he forgot his own wildness. She could only hope she hadn't caused him any harm – that he'd keep his distance from people – people like Shannon and Jimmy Blythe. People like Daniel.

She bit her lip, longed for Dad; for his reassuring hand on her shoulder, telling her she could make things right now. That she was brave. That Bird would be OK.

A chill wind rose out of nowhere, whipped up the forest floor; created a tsunami of whispering leaves. If Dad's voice was there at all, the wind had stolen it. And she knew, didn't she? Dad would never have taken Bird home in the first place . . .

She reached for Bird, but Bird fluttered up into the waving skirts of the evergreen, disappeared among the vivid green fronds. Billie stared after him. Waited. The rain stopped. Wind whined through bare branches. Late-shrivelled leaves whirled downwards; settled.

That was it then. Decision made.

Bird had chosen.

The chill air stung her cheeks; wormed its way inside her coat, a ball of ice against her chest where Bird had nestled just a few hours earlier. But this *was* the right thing. It was.

'Bye, Bird,' she whispered, her words lost to the wind, hurled high into the tree canopy. 'Be happy being free.'

She took the lid off the still wriggling lunchbox and tucked it in among the swing-tree roots; heaved her backpack on to her shoulder. It felt heavier than before, like it was full of stones. She turned, walked away. Her feet dragged in the sodden leaf-carpet. She steeled herself not to look back at every twig-snap or rustle in the undergrowth, stopping just once as the swoop of a starling made her heart leap.

By the time Billie reached the far edge of Tanglewood, the sky was thick with the promise of more rain. The wind drove grey clouds across the sky. They clustered together above the play park, darkening. Full of storm stories. Bird's spindly tree hideout bent forward in the wind; dripped the last of the earlier rain. A final thin leaf was torn from it as Billie passed, twisted to the floor in front of her. Her eyes blurred. But she mustn't be sad. Bird was free. And she had helped him. Now, she could concentrate on getting to Dad. When she found him, she'd tell him all about Bird. Maybe they'd come to look for him in Tanglewood, the two of them. Together. Billie would have a raven story of her own to share. She felt the tug of a smile, looked away from Bird's tree and walked on.

A small figure sat hunched at the top of the slide. Nell. How come she was out in this weather, and all by herself again?

Nell with her button-bright eyes; her questions. Billie couldn't deal with either, not today. She put her head down; hurried on past.

Icy balls of hail bounced on to the pavement outside Mr Chatterjee's shop with its Sunday-dark windows. Billie pulled up her hood. The wind threw it back again. She left it, let the hail sting her scalp and numb her thoughts. As the flats came into view, her stomach squirmed as if the lunchbox worms were in there. What kind of Sunday was it at home? Daniel would be there now, sucking the air out of the room. Like it was all his own, and Billie and Mam shouldn't dare to breathe. Anger tightened Billie's stomach.

The worry worms tumbled, crawled into her throat, tried to burst out through her chest. She held out her hands, snatched at the hailstones, hurled them in the air again. She thought of Bird, tucked away in Tanglewood. She *was* happy for him. She *was*. And he was best out of Daniel's way, that was for sure. But she missed him already. Without him there was only Daniel and the ice-splinter silences, the stifling air. The Dad-shaped hole in her heart.

The sky spoke of storms to come. Hardly the weather for running away.

'I'm going anyway,' she told the sky. 'As soon as I can. Whatever you have to say about it.

'I'm going to find my dad.'

TWELVE

Next morning, Daniel left early for his four-day trip; was gone before Billie was up and dressed for school. But his presence hung heavy in every room. Something had upset him last night: his voice had rumbled through Billie's bedroom walls like approaching thunder. Billie had lain awake for hours, poker-straight, straining to make out what he was saying; listening for Mam in between the throb of Daniel's words, checking for changes in the rhythm of her voice – any sign that she was upset. Scared.

Billie heard her name; heard it bounce around between them. There'd been a scuffling noise – then the loud silence with its splinter edges. Billie tossed and turned. Should she get up, go and see if Mam was OK? Would that just make things worse? Her mind and body felt empty; useless. Like she had floated away and left them there like discarded shells on a beach.

Eventually, Daniel's heavy Sunday night snores rumbled in the darkness. Mam's tiptoe-feet in the hallway; the click

114

of the bathroom light. Billie fumbled for her bedside lamp, forced her heavy limbs over the side of the bed. She eased open her bedroom door, saw Mam haloed in the lit bathroom doorway, bent over the sink.

Her door shifted in the draught from her window, made a creak of complaint. Mam turned, reached for a towel and held it to her face. She'd been crying. Billie knew she had.

'Mam?' Billie whispered. 'Are you all right?'

'I'm fine,' Mam whispered back. She held a finger to her lip. She pulled the light switch; plunged the hall into darkness.

'Honestly, Mam?' Billie said. 'Are you sure?'

'I've said, haven't I, Billie? Now back to bed with you. Before you wake Daniel. He's got an early start in the morning.' She moved closer, touched Billie's arm. Her face was skeletal in the gloom, all hollows and shadows in the weak light leaking through her bedroom door. Were there any new marks there? Impossible to know. But Billie *knew*.

Mam ushered her into her bedroom. For a moment, Billie thought she might stay, tuck her back into bed like when she was small, afraid of midnight dream-monsters or the moon shadows dancing on her walls. Instead, she scuttled away like a startled rabbit, closing the door behind her so that it made no sound at all.

Billie had never felt more alone. She thought of Bird in the woods. Of their flight together. Of how it felt to have a friend.

She stuffed her head under her pillow and let the tears come. Finally, she slept.

But in the morning, her head was full of fog and her insides felt hollow.

Mam, judging by the puffiness around her eyes; the wisps of hair straggling from her new 'office up-do', had not slept much either. The kettle was cold. There was no smell of toast. No smell of bacon, either. Daniel must be long gone, but his presence still hung heavy in the cold room.

'You OK, Mam?' Billie said. Her worry worms wriggled in her throat, made her voice wobble.

Mam didn't seem to notice. 'Just running late, love,' she said. She planted a quick kiss on Billie's cheek. She grabbed two apples from the bowl on the side and pressed one into Billie's hand. 'For your lunchbox. Cheese and salad stuff in the fridge for your sandwiches, OK?'

Billie nodded. Although it wasn't. Nothing was.

Dad used to be in charge of lunchboxes: fat, snug-wrapped sandwiches in silver foil, an apple, redder than her hair, one of her favourite bubbly chocolate bars or the golden flapjacks that Mam made. Now and then, there'd be a surprise tucked alongside. A note, or a flower from their garden pressed between tissue. A speckled feather. Once, a fragment of sky-blue robin's egg, tissue-thin and beautiful.

According to Daniel, Billie was old enough to make her own sandwiches. Which was true – although not the point. To begin with, Mam had just smiled and carried on doing it for her. Now it was mainly down to Billie. Mam didn't bake flapjacks any more. And she bought green apples, not red. No prizes for guessing why that was. Daniel was even in charge of apples.

Mam fussed around the kitchen, opening drawers, pushing things aside.

'For goodness' sake,' she said. 'Where *is* it – my phone?' She looked at Billie, her eyes full of a wild panic that Billie had never seen there before. She rushed from the room, reappeared a minute later, phone in hand and far too much relief on her face.

Billie swallowed soggy cereal past the ball of worry worms. Mam never even remembered where her phone *was* when Dad was around. And Dad never remembered to charge his. This phone obsession was Daniel again. Always texting or ringing Mam – checking in, Mam said.

More like checking *on* her, Billie thought. Always here, even when he wasn't. And not in a good way. Why couldn't Mam see what he was doing?

Billie stared at Mam. No point in saying anything. Words wouldn't get past the roadblock in her throat. Mam wouldn't hear her anyway. Billie knew that now. She could only hear Daniel. Billie looked away, poked at the Weetabix in her bowl, now a thick clump like the one in her throat. She threw down her spoon, squeezed the tears back behind her eyes.

Mam leaned in, tilted Billie's chin with one finger. But she didn't see. Didn't ask.

'Billie? Sandwiches, yes? And don't forget your key. You'll be home before me today. OK?' She smiled a nothing smile, tucked her stray hair behind her ear. There was a new crease-line between her eyebrows and her face was painted on with thick make-up. She didn't look real. Didn't look *here*.

'Yes. OK,' Billie muttered. Although it wasn't. Nothing was. Dad was gone and Daniel had been chipping her mam away, piece by piece. Soon there'd be nothing left of Mam either.

Bird had been a distraction – made her feel useful for once. Made her feel a bit closer to Dad.

Now Bird was gone too. And with him, the tiny new feeling of hope that had uncurled inside Billie like a spring seed.

She had annoyed Daniel yesterday and Mam had suffered for it, she was sure. What if her running away made things even worse? Perhaps she should be trying to persuade Mam to leave too. Maybe after last night, she'd see sense . . .

'Mam . . .'

'Gotta go, love,' Mam said. 'And so should you.' She grabbed her phone from the bench. Her face fell.

Daniel. It had to be.

'Just you and me later, Billie. Girls' night. We'll talk then, love.'

But they wouldn't. Not really. Not about the things that needed saying.

Mam tapped her phone, put it to her ear, greeted him like nothing had happened. Like she loved him. The door closed behind her. Another closed in Billie's heart.

She didn't bother to make sandwiches. The worry worms had multiplied overnight. Their cold bodies jostled for space inside her, filled her stomach and chest. There was no room for food.

She missed Bird. Had she got things wrong with him,

wrong too, and Bird was waiting for her under the tree canopy; cold, hungry and lonely?

Billie pushed the image away. She faced another day of nudging, whispering classmates. More hours of trying to focus on lessons while her brain fizzed and fogged and fretted. The thought of Bird happily roosting with new raven friends in the Tanglewood trees – that might just get her through. Make her feel less alone.

The faces of so-called 'best friends' from her old school flickered across her mind, their faces in and out of focus like the old wartime film reels they'd watched together in class.

There had been hugs and promises that last day, a few messages since from Maggie and Niall. A birthday card from Hazel. But then, nothing. No more messages. No replies to her own. Mam said that was the way of things for children – life moved on quickly, that was all. It wouldn't be about Dad. Or Billie. It didn't mean anything.

Mam was wrong. It meant something very important.

It meant there was no point in making friends.

The day went by in a blur. Books. Blackboard. Whiteboard. Mr Freeman's lilting voice that once might have held her attention with its musical rhythm, its way of smoothing out the puzzles of fractions and semi-colons and making her feel like she was right there: hunkered down in a World War Two air-raid shelter or creeping inside an Egyptian tomb. These days, he might as well have been speaking Egyptian; writing on the board in hieroglyphics. Even the stupid jokes and jibes of Jimmy and his stupid friends seemed far away; nothing to do with Billie. The lunchtime library brought no respite from the whorl of worry. She hid herself away in the furthest corner, behind the rows of children's encyclopaedias where layers of dust confirmed that she was most likely to be left alone this time too. Her eyes ran along the thick spines, stopped at 'S to T', its dark blue and silver lettering unmuted by dust. She pictured the spread of dark sky, spinning planets and silver constellations; thought briefly of taking it down again. Didn't.

She curled up on a beanbag by the window and chewed at the skin around her thumb.

What would happen next time Daniel got upset?

Should Billie go through with her plan to run away? Or should she stay, make sure Mam was OK? But then, what could she do there? She wasn't brave enough to protect Mam or even herself. She just made things worse. She was no use at all . . .

And what about Bird, all alone in Tanglewood? Was *he* safe? Had she just made things worse for him too? Dark visions crowded her head. Bird, bloodied and limping, attacked by the raven community, or chased by starlings because he carried the alien scent of human touch

Should she go back to Tanglewood and check on him?

Should she run to Dad all by herself like she planned, or was there a better plan? Someone else, someone anywhere, who she could trust to help her?

Where are you, Dad? she whispered into the windowpane. *Tell me what to do.*

She stared past the jostling blur of navy and red bodies in the playground, searched the sky, as if for answers.

Nothing.

No sky writing. No sky stories to comfort her. No black bird soaring free.

Just wide grey nothing as far as she could see.

Even the sky had abandoned her.

THIRTEEN

Billie heard them before she saw them. And she knew. Knew by the rhythm, the rise and fall of laughter, raucous as crows fighting over a carcass. Knew by the roars, the silences in between, they were up to no good, and at someone else's expense.

A huddle of navy and red by the play park. Laughter rose and fell. It wasn't the good kind. Shannon's shrill notes rang. Billie made out Jimmy's spiky blond head; the lash of a dark ponytail – his older sister Millie's, no doubt. Those two were joined at the hip for some reason. And she was almost as mean as Shannon. There were others: two boys that Billie didn't recognise: one small and hooded, hovering at the edge of the group, one tall, all knees and elbows and razored hair. They hustled, shoulder to shoulder in a squashed circle, leaned in; as if watching something. Or someone. The spindly tree rose above them, seemed to tremble in the air. Bird's tree . . .

A stick, waving in the air. Heads flung back in unison,

a sudden burst of clownish cheering.

Billie's worry worms whorled and whipped and pressed upwards. She felt sick. Who, or *what*, were they taunting this time? She wanted to turn, find another way home. She couldn't. She was sick of it. Sick of always feeling scared.

She rushed forward. 'Hey!' she shouted. 'Hey! What are you doing?'

Heads over shoulders; stares. Smirks. More laughter. A glimpse of movement – pale hair, red wellies, as the huddle of navy and red bodies parted slightly.

Nell.

'Leave her alone,' Billie heard herself shout. She stopped just short of the group, feet planted on the ground like the strong roots of an oak, even though she felt more like Bird's quivering sapling.

'So *scared*, aren't I?' Shannon flicked her ponytail over her shoulder; smirked. 'Get lost, Ginger,' she said. 'Mind your own.' She spat a grey lump of chewing gum on the ground by Billie's feet. Like she was nothing. Like Nell was nothing.

Billie's fists curled into balls. 'Let her out,' she hissed. She stepped closer, tried to peer over the shoulder of the smaller boy. 'Nell,' she shouted. 'You OK? Come on. I'll take you home.'

Jimmy stepped forward, pushed at her shoulder, stick still in hand. 'Oooh, what's this?' he said, his mouth stretched into a snake-grin. 'Little misfits sticking together, eh? Should have guessed. Silly me.' His smile vanished. He pointed the stick close to her chest, prodded her jacket. 'Do one, OK?'

Daniel. He was just like Daniel. A bully. A stupid bully.

Rage flashed through Billie's body, hot and fierce. Her worry worms shrank from it.

She grabbed the end of the stick. '*Get* off me,' she hissed.

Jimmy held on to the other end. His eyes flashed with something Billie couldn't quite read. Then he clasped one hand to his head, glanced over his shoulder at the group as if to make sure they were listening. 'Or what?' he said. 'Gonna beat me up, jail-bird girl? Like father like daughter, is it?' He stuffed a fist in his mouth, shook his body in mock trembling.

Billie's fists balled. She wanted to punch him, see him flat on his back on the muddy ground with the worms and the windblown litter. But would that make her just like Daniel?

Rise above it, Billie. Ignore them. That's what Dad would say. *They have a wildness inside them trying to get out; they're hurting somewhere you can't see . . .*

125

She twisted the stick away, surprised at the strength that surged from her chest and into her arms. 'You don't know anything about my dad,' she said, staring Jimmy in the eye. 'Or me. But seeing as you think it's funny to pick on people just for the fun of it, it's you lot that should be locked up, not him.' She pushed past him and shouldered her way between a shocked Millie and the hooded boy, who moved away with a nervous glance at Jimmy.

Nell stood stiff as a soldier, chin in the air. Her duffle coat was balled up in her arms, wrapped in a striped sweater, slight body shaking under a shiver-thin shirt. 'I looked after him for you, Billie,' she said, the glimmer of held-back tears starting in her eyes. She blinked them away; stood taller, shook her head. 'I kept him warm and I covered him and I never let them idiots hurt him.' A grey, clawed foot slipped from the bundle she held, scrabbled against her shirt. She tucked it back with one hand.

'Bird!' Billie gasped. Her heart leaped in her chest, banged against her ribs. 'Is he OK, Nell? Are you? Was it him they were trying to . . .'

She knelt in front of Nell, who eased the bird-bundle into her arms. Bird's black head pushed its way out. A black bead eye stared at Billie, blinked. She hugged him to her.

'Brave, that's what you are, Nell,' Billie said. 'Super brave.' She stood, glared at Jimmy, then at Shannon, ignoring the slip-slide-squirm of worry worms returning. 'You lot think you're so tough, but you're all cowards!' she announced, surprised at the boldness in her own voice.

'Yeah,' Nell shouted, her hazelnut eyes dark now, big and round as conkers. 'Wait till me nan hears about this. You'll be proper for it then!'

Jimmy stepped forward, pushed his face close to Billie's, then Nell's. 'Terrified, aren't I?' he said. 'That batty old biddy!' He threw back his head, laughed. 'What's she gonna do? Knit me some handcuffs! Clobber me with a bag of birdseed? Run me down with her purple Nan-mobile?'

Shannon's screech-owl laughter cut through his own, ended in a sneer. 'Got any more terrifying family then, have you? Kept them out of sight if you have!' she said.

Millie laughed. 'Yeah. Invisible. Like your mam and dad.'

'I heard she's only got a mam and even *she* doesn't want her most of the time.' Jimmy sniffed away pretend tears. 'That right, squirt?'

'You shut up,' Nell said.

'Yes,' Billie said, stepping in front of Nell and Bird. 'Shut up. Leave her alone and clear off.'

'Or what?' Jimmy sniggered.

'C'mon, Jimmy,' knees-and-elbows-boy said. 'It's just stupid loner kids and a half-dead bird that's probably got fleas. Boring. Let's go.'

'Yeah, let's go.' Millie pulled at his sleeve. 'Dad texted. It's dinner time. You know what he said . . .'

Jimmy glanced at her, then at Shannon, who stood chewing on the end of her ponytail. He straightened up, leaned close to Billie's face. 'Lucky for you,' he said, his voice slithering like a snake, 'I'm starving.' He hoisted his stick over his shoulder. 'But if I see that scrawny bird round here again . . . Well, let's just say, I'd better not. Ravens, they're bad news; bad luck. An' I reckon they got germs from all them dead things they eat. Disgusting.'

'Yeah. We don't want 'em round here,' Shannon added. She pulled more chewing gum from between her teeth, stretched it, curled it back inside her mouth. 'Scavengers, they are.'

Jimmy nodded. 'Got it, misfits?' he said, twirling his stick in the air. He turned and walked away, dragging it along the metal bars of the fence, so that his angry music echoed across the play park as he and his band of followers swaggered away. The smallest boy looked back for a moment, slowed his steps, then ran to catch up with the rest.

FOURTEEN

Billie watched them go, felt her shoulders drop as they grew smaller and smaller. She realised she was shaking. She turned her attention to Nell, whose pale hair lay dark with rain against her head, making her look smaller, younger. But there was something about her eyes that Billie hadn't noticed before. Something – older than her ten years. Something brave.

'They didn't hurt you, did they?' Billie asked. 'I mean, with that stick or anything.'

Nell shook her head. Tiny drops of water flew from her sodden hair.

'Them kids never *do* anything. They just think they're big an' clever if they say nasty stuff and scare people. And birds and cats – anything,' she said, head cocked wisely to one side now. Her eyes met Billie's. 'But they only act big 'cos they feel small, that's what Nan says.'

Billie smiled. She nodded; felt a flicker of longing to meet Nell's nan; to tell her about Dad.

About Daniel.

But no. *We keep our business to ourselves in this family.* Daniel's voice, a low rumble through her bedroom wall. Growing louder, deeper, like thunder moving closer. *We don't go blabbing about it. Not to anyone, right? Right?*

Daniel felt small too. Billie didn't care. But she still couldn't tell, couldn't risk making Daniel angry. She had to keep Mam safe.

Anyway, she wasn't going to trust Nell's nan. She wasn't about to trust anyone but herself. Not even Nell. Even though she had protected Bird and Billie was actually starting to like her . . .

Bird wriggled inside his duffle-coat refuge. Bird was her priority now. Her only real friend.

'C'mon, Nell,' she said, nodding towards the play-park bench. 'Let's sit there and check on Bird. Then I'll walk home with you, OK?'

Nell followed, silent for once as Billie unwrapped the coat bundle on her lap.

Bird's head popped out. He blinked. Squawked. Wriggled his wings free of the heavy fabric and flapped them. He hopped up on to Billie's wrist where he began to groom himself, pulling long wing-feathers one by one through his beak.

He was fine. He really was fine. Billie's shoulders relaxed. Warmth spread though her body. Her friend was back.

But she shouldn't be glad, she knew. Not really.

'I left you in Tanglewood, Bird,' she said. 'What are you doing out here again? It's not safe.' She turned to Nell. 'What happened?'

Nell slid her coat from Billie's lap, felt around in the folds. She shrugged.

'Think he was looking for you,' she said. 'He was waiting on the path: hiding under that little tree, but it weren't very good hiding. I seen him from the top of the slide. An' I seen the stick kids coming too. So I went and got him, didn't I?'

She produced a crumpled paper package from one of her coat pockets. 'Nan's blueberry muffins,' she said, showing squashed blue and yellow remains inside the paper package. 'Want some?'

Billie shook her head. 'No. Thanks,' she said. 'Not hungry.'

Nell shrugged again. 'Bird likes 'em, don't you, Bird?' She looked up at Billie, round eyes serious. 'That's how I got him to let me pick him up,' she said. She stuffed a flattened chunk of blue and yellow sponge into her mouth, held out a blueberry and a few crumbs in the palm of her hand.

Bird reached forward, picked out the blueberry and weighed it in his beak for a moment before trying to tuck it up inside Billie's coat cuff.

Billie laughed. 'Look at that,' she said. 'I think he's saving it till later!'

Nell nodded slowly. 'Clever birds, them ravens,' she said. She studied Bird, her small face serious again.

A changeable face, Billie thought. A face as full of stories as the sky.

'Why do you think them kids hate them when they ain't done nothing 'cept being birds?' Nell asked.

Billie ran a finger over Bird's back. Nell was growing on her. She wasn't like the other kids at school. She knew things. Understood things. Perhaps it was because of all the questions she asked. Or all the books she read. She thought for a moment. 'You know those stories you like . . . in books –'

'An' the ones me nan tells,' Nell cut in.

'Yes,' Billie said. 'Those too. Well, my dad said there are lots of stories about ravens. Stories from long ago and from different parts of the world. Some good. Some bad. People made things up, he said, because of how big and black these birds are, and especially because they get seen around dead things – animals and birds – which is just their food. He said people call a group of them "an unkindness" of ravens. Which is rubbish, because they're clever and beautiful and kind and just doing what they need to stay alive . . .'

Nell stared at Billie. 'Does your dad know all them raven stories? When's he comin' home again? Can I listen to them too, when he does, like?'

Billie looked away. 'Dad's . . . he'll be back soon,' she said. 'I'm not sure exactly when. But I'm going to look at his bird books and find out more about ravens – find out how to look after Bird – just for a bit longer. I'm going to work out how to help him go back to being a proper wild bird, safe from people that might hurt him. And we could find the raven stories too – there might be some in Dad's books, or in the library.' She could search on the internet too. She wasn't allowed to use the laptop at home any more. Another Daniel rule. Not even Mam was supposed to use it. *He* needed it, for work.

'I can look s'well, Billie,' Nell said, jiggling on the seat. 'At school. An' I can ask Nan about looking after Bird.'

Billie smiled at Nell's eager face, but she rested a hand on her arm. 'Good,' she said. 'Only you can't tell – about Bird. Not even your nan. OK? Otherwise, they'll make me let him go and the stick kids will get him.'

'But your dad likes birds, don't he?' Nell said, studying Bird's enormous toes and tracing his nails with her finger. 'He'll let you keep him, won't he? He'll help him?'

Billie looked away.

'Like I said, he's still away . . .'

Nell rested her chin on her hands and looked up at Billie. 'That girl with the chewing gum – she said your dad's in prison and he's *never* comin' out. She said he's a bad person that stole money and it was in the papers an' everything.' She pulled a blueberry from her squashed muffin, held it out for Bird. 'He don't sound like a bad person, though,' she said, locking eyes with Billie. 'He sounds nice.' She stuffed the last of her cake into her mouth. 'That girl – Shannon – she says stuff about me mam too.' She straightened up, swallowed, locked eyes with Billie. 'Unkind things that ain't true. She told lies about me, so no one wants to be my friend.' Her red wellies lifted, fell. Lifted, fell. She shrugged. 'It's OK though, I s'pose. 'Cos I got me nan.'

Billie stared off into the sky. Clouds, clumped together, jostling for space, raggedy edges. More rain was on its way then. Maybe even a storm. A swirl of wind lifted Bird's feathers. He tucked his head inside the crook of Billie's arm.

Billie's thoughts swirled too. How could she explain about Dad to Nell? She couldn't really explain him to herself. He *had* taken money that he shouldn't have done. He'd told her. He had been scared. Made a terrible mistake. But he wasn't a criminal. He wasn't, was he? He was Dad. Kind, gentle, honest Dad who loved her.

Dad who had stopped writing.

'He *is* nice,' she said. 'My dad. He just . . . he just . . .' Words balled up in her throat, stuck there: clumped and ragged and muddled, like the clouds. She moved her hand from Nell's coat, registering for the first time how damp it was. She swallowed, cleared her throat.

'We need to go. Get warm and dry . . .'

Nell's feet stilled. She twisted the cake paper in her hands, sprinkled the last of the crumbs into her palm for Bird. 'Gentle bird, ain't he?' she said. 'Even with that big, hooky beak.'

Billie nodded. 'C'mon then, Nell.'

Nell stuffed the paper package in her pocket. 'Me mam,' she said. 'She's gone away too.'

'Why?' Billie asked. 'Where?'

Nell sat on her hands, began swinging her feet again. She shrugged. 'She just couldn't stay, that's what Nan says. Stayin' made her sick.'

She looked up at Billie, brown eyes clear; full of a certainty Billie remembered inside herself from long ago. 'She gave me to Nan 'cos she loves me, that's what Nan says.'

'What's she like?' Billie asked. 'Your mam?'

Nell wiped her hands on her jeans, brushed crumbs from her sleeve. Bird hopped down from Billie's shoulder, began collecting them from the muddy path. Nell watched him, the trace of a smile on her face. 'I were just a tiny bairn when she went away. I only remember her in bits. She had silvery earrings that kind of sang when she moved, and she smelled of lemons. I stayed with me auntie Lou for a bit then, over South Hetton. But then she got married an' went to live in Spain, so I went to live with Pete and Mark, near me old school. Foster care, like. They were all right, Pete and Mark. Only they couldn't keep me forever and that's when me nan said, "Enough's enough. The bairn stays with me, whatever anyone's got to say about me age."'

Goodness. That was what Billie had seen in Nell's eyes. Courage. She really *was* brave . . .

And Nan got better by the minute. If only *Billie* had a nan still living, perhaps things might be different.

She felt the nudge of Nell's arm.

'Your dad and my mam – it's like with the ravens, ain't

it, Billie?' Nell said, straightening up. 'Like them kids, saying mean stuff that ain't true?'

Tears prickled the back of Billie's eyes. She looked down at Bird, nodded.

'Yes. Just like the ravens,' she said. 'Stories. Made-up stuff. People thinking they know things when they don't. It's not fair. But maybe it doesn't matter if we know the real truth ourselves.'

But then again, she thought, other people needed to know the truth about Daniel, didn't they? To make him stop . . . And they needed to know the truth about Dad too, so they didn't hate him and shut her out.

Why was everything so complicated?

A sudden beam of sunlight glanced off Bird's ink-black feathers. They glistened blue, purple and green. 'Like oil in a puddle,' she whispered, pointing. 'A little bit of rainbow left on the roadside; or maybe a sprinkle of stardust captured by the rain, just because it can . . .'

Nell stared at her, eyes conker-round again.

'One of my dad's stories,' Billie said. Warmth flashed across her chest. Her dad saw beauty everywhere. It was one of the things she loved about him the most. One of the things she missed the most.

Would he be the same when he got out of prison? Or

would the grey boxy building; the darkness there, have pushed behind his eyes, changed how he saw the world forever?

Nell twisted her mouth to one side. 'So he's definitely coming home then? Your dad. Only Nabil in my class said your mam's got a new boyfriend now, 'cos his dad met him in the pub, like, and he said *he* was your dad now, an' all. David or Darren or summat? Is that wrong, an' all?'

Billie's jaw tightened. Daniel would never *ever* be her dad. How *dare* he say that?

'It's *Daniel*,' she shouted, wishing she could spit the letters one by one on to the ground like pieces of Shannon's chewing gum. 'And he's a massive liar and I hate him.'

Bird flinched, lifted his wings and fluttered up on to Billie's shoulder. He peered round at her, head almost upside down. One liquorice eye blinked its clockwork blink.

'Sorry, Bird,' Billie whispered. She turned her face towards him, pressed back angry tears, felt the brush of his soft, dusty feathers against her cheek.

That was it. She was getting in touch with Dad now, whatever it took. Even if she had to hammer on the great, barred prison gate until someone let her in.

And now, perhaps, she'd have her friend Bird to keep her company along the way.

She stood up, tried to coax Bird back into the safety of her jacket. He was having none of it, preferred to stay perched on her shoulder, head turning this way and that as if to survey the area for safety.

'Like Dickon's raven,' Nell said, her gappy grin lighting up her face. 'In *The Secret Garden*. Remember, Billie? Did you read that one?'

She nodded; thinking about how she'd loved that book; loved the neglected garden that had bloomed anew when lonely Mary and Dickon showed it love. Loved that the garden had helped Mary to make friends and to feel happy; helped sickly Colin to walk and run free among the wind and flowers. How it broke down the walls between him and his sad, guilty father.

'A robin!' she said. 'A robin led Mary to the secret garden, didn't it?'

Nell beamed, nodded. She jumped down from the set with a clump of wellies. 'Yes,' she said. 'It made Mary follow it, showed her the door all hidden with ivy.'

'Like it knew,' Billie whispered into her coat. 'Like it was telling her what to do.'

She wrapped her arms across her chest, held Bird snuggly against her heart.

She saw it now: Bird had come back for her; come

back to find her where they first met.

So maybe it wasn't *her* that found *him* that first frosty Saturday. Maybe it was the other way round. Her blood was in her ears, pushing heat into her cheeks. Because maybe, just maybe, this wild raven had come to help, just like Mary's robin.

Was that even possible, outside of books? Billie doubted it. Except, a dad who read bird music in the sky and spotted stars in puddles – well, he might just be the one to make it happen.

And if he *had*, that must mean something very important indeed.

She needed to get home. Needed to think. But suddenly, everything seemed clearer. Dad was trying to reach her; *wanted* her to come to him. Excitement fluttered in her chest.

Nell was beaming up at her, bright belief in her nut-brown eyes. Somehow, Bird and Nell were connected too. He had led Nell into Billie's life. Today, Nell had been a friend to him, and to her . . .

Billie smiled back at her.

'Let's go, Nell,' she said. 'Storm is coming. I'll walk you to yours. Then I'll know where you live.'

FIFTEEN

The rain was back with a vengeance by the time Nell stopped outside a tiny, faded red-brick house squeezed on the end of a row of others just like it. This one had a surprisingly purple front door and a small, square van parked alongside it. That was purple too. Its large, round headlamps and curved bumper gave it the appearance of a face. A cheerful face, out of place in the rainy street. Just like the purple door. A red flower had been painted on the bonnet. That was faded too, like the house, leaving only three petals visible as if the wind had taken the others.

'That's Florence,' Nell announced, following Billie's gaze. She grinned her gappy grin; wiped rain from her nose. 'Me nan, she loves purple.'

'Right,' Billie said, wondering whether Nan would turn out to have purple hair like an old lady in a poem she'd once read at school. 'Does it . . . work? I mean, does she drive it?'

Nell nodded. 'Sometimes. When there's somewhere

special to go. Florence, she's a bit old, so you can't work her too hard, got to save her energy for when it's really needed. Same as for Nan.' The gappy grin widened. 'She's cool, Florence. She's got beds an' a cooker an' a kind of separate room that you make with curtains. Want to see inside? Me nan'll let you. Wait here a minute. I'll get the keys.'

Nell spun round, headed for the front door, wellies scuffing on the path.

'Nell, no. Wait. I can't – Bird . . . remember?'

'Nan prob'ly won't notice him – not under your coat. She's waitin' for her new glasses. Anyway, she wouldn't mind. She don't mind most things, Nan.'

Billie sighed. She checked the window for a glimpse of purple hair or squinting window-eyes; walked closer to Nell. 'But like I said,' she whispered, 'Bird has to be a secret, Nell. Just our secret, you and me.'

Nell plonked herself down on the wet doorstep, began trying to pull off her wellies. Her face brightened. 'Like Mary's garden,' she said. 'Like in the book.'

'Exactly like that,' Billie said. 'Bird has to stay hidden away.'

Nell gave a solemn nod and pushed open the door. Apparently, locking doors was another thing that Nan didn't mind about.

'Call for us tomorrow,' she said over her shoulder. 'An' bring "the secret". Bye!'

The purple door swung shut behind her, leaving Billie and Bird alone in the rain-swept street. She stared at the closed door, imagined a warm hallway, a kitchen that smelled of baking. She saw herself sitting cross-legged on Nell's bed, spilling out the worry worms. Telling her about Daniel. About Dad's letters. About everything. Telling her about her plan.

Nell making it all OK with more of her nan's wise sayings . . .

She imagined the lightness of it. Of having a friend.

Nell was brave. She had proved that today. Billie knew she could be trusted to keep Bird safe, to keep him a secret. But her other secrets: they might be too heavy for Nell to hold. And she didn't really know her, not properly. She'd known her Green Lane School friends for years, but they'd still drifted away like smoke when she really needed them.

Bird squirmed against her, let out an uneasy squawk.

'It's all right, Bird,' Billie said. 'We're going home.' She turned away from Nell's door, looked up and down the wet, blustery street.

Which way *was* home? Billie wasn't entirely sure. But

surely that was a trace of Mr Chatterjee's fried chicken on the wind. She'd follow that . . .

It turned out that Nell lived only two streets from there. Which was just as well. The wind was fiercer by the minute, driving the rain into her face like cold needles, trying to push her back three steps for every two she took. Bird was still, apparently sleeping, and oblivious to the weather. Billie was relieved when the grey bulk of the flats came into view. This time, her worry worms were quiet. Yes, she had to smuggle Bird past Mam, but there was no Daniel. Today, she could breathe all the indoor air she wanted. And Mam, she might be a bit more – Mam.

Might talk about Dad.

She appeared, cloth in hand, as Billie stood dripping inside the front door; insisting she go straight into a warm shower.

'And leave those wet clothes on your chair,' she said, ducking back around the kitchen door. 'Your jacket too. They'll need to go in the washer as soon as I'm done with these cupboards. Filthy as well as soaked, by the look of it.'

Cleaning. Mam was always cleaning. Even though nothing was dirty. Before Daniel, she never even owned a pair of rubber gloves. Now they seemed to be permanently glued to her hands. Daniel saw germs everywhere. Daniel liked things neat. And it was Mam's job to make them that way, never his own.

Mam's head round the door again:

'Oh, and I've taped some card over that crack in your window – seeing as the tape didn't hold. It's just till Daniel's back. He'll fix it properly then. He's promised. He's just been so busy, love.'

The wind was already pushing at Mam's temporary repair, making the card bulge forward in the middle, distorting the bowl of cereal pictured there, so that it looked as if it might propel cornflakes around the room at any moment. Billie bet that wind would have Mam's handiwork beaten well before bedtime.

She didn't register how cold and wet she'd been until she was wrapped in her dressing gown. She shivered, pulled it closer around herself. She looked at Bird, who was pecking at the still, glass eyes of her old teddy bear on his chest-of-drawers perch. Among the worry worms, something new and beautiful jostled for space, like a flower was growing there, opening its petals to the light. Bird was back. She hadn't imagined that moment on the Tanglewood swing. It was real. She and Bird were connected. And Bird was connected to Dad. Billie felt the stretch of a smile for the second time that day.

The flower in her chest. It felt like hope.

Bird was meant to be here. She knew that now. She had been right to bring him in from the wild.

Bird flew back to her shoulder, pulled a strand of her wet hair though his beak, flicked rainwater against her neck. She shivered again, she'd best get warm and dry. Couldn't afford to catch a cold. She had important plans.

She'd have to take Bird with her into the bathroom – Mam might appear at any moment for her wet things.

She scooped him up, draped a towel over him.

'Don't wriggle, and don't squawk,' she said. 'Just be quiet for a few seconds, OK?'

She hurried down the corridor, bare feet silent on the lino; breathed a sigh of relief once safely behind the locked bathroom door. She set Bird down on the linen basket, cushioned by his thick towel. She pulled the shower curtain closed, reached round, and turned on the water, one eye on Bird. She had to hope he wouldn't get too scared, get into one of his noisy panics.

He barely seemed to notice the shower, was fascinated instead by the drip-drip-glint of water from one of the taps on the sink. Just as Billie thought it safe to step into the shower, he took off, landing first on the shelf above the sink, where he toppled the toothbrush mug and sent toothbrushes and toothpaste skittering towards the plughole below. A quick fluster of feathers and a single squawk of alarm, and he settled himself on the side of the sink. He gave Mam's pink soap an exploratory peck, making it slither after the toothbrushes, then turned his attention to the water droplets, trying to catch them as they fell.

Billie listened, strained to hear above the hiss of the shower. Was Mam outside? Had she heard anything? She held her breath.

No. Nothing. She breathed out. Shot Bird a nervous glance.

He seemed happy: captivated now by glimpses of himself in the shiny metal tap. But Billie had best get done quick-snap . . .

The steamy shower-burst was wonderful on her cold skin. She closed her eyes – just for a second or two, let the warm rivers tumble over her face and hair. She opened them just as Bird's black wings lifted above the shower rail, feet dangling like landing gear of an aircraft as he searched for a perch. He chose the top of the shower rail, curled his clawed toes around it, slip-swayed on the wet metal for a moment; thought again. Next thing Billie knew, he was in the bath with her, splash-paddling in the swirling water around her feet; flapping his wings like a sparrow bathing in a puddle.

'Bird,' Billie said. 'Honestly!'

Despite the shock – and Bird looking rather too interested in her toes, Billie felt the pull of another smile.

She stepped out of the bath just as Bird made a definite dive for her left big toe, slung her towel around herself, and scooped Bird on to her lap.

A rap at the door. Mam.

'Billie? You nearly done, love? I've put soup on for us . . .'

A double knock.

'Billie?'

Bird's feet skitter-scratched and scrabbled in alarm as he tried to balance on the side of the bath, lost his grip and slid back down into the spin-swirl of water near the plughole. This time, his panicked squawk was LOUD.

'Billie – what on earth was that?'

'Nothing, Mam,' Billie shouted, hastily scooping Bird back inside his towel, muffling his disgruntled squeaks. 'Just a weird screeching noise in the pipes or something. Sounds like there's an angry bird in there.' She turned off the shower, whispered into the folds of the towel. 'Please, Bird. Shhh, now. Shhh.'

'This place,' Mam mumbled from behind the door.

148

'Right, well, come on, love. Let's get that soup before it spoils.'

Probably too late for that, Billie thought, as she opened up Bird's towel and tried to find a dry corner. Mam might have made some fresh, she supposed; maybe used one of Dad's old recipes. She could hope. But more likely it was the cheap stuff Daniel insisted was *more economical and frees up your mam's time for things she wants to do*. Only it didn't. Unless you counted working all day and then running round after Daniel. Mam had no free time any more. She certainly had no time for the new friends she'd been making. What had happened to Mel from the office, with her big hoop earrings and super-loud laugh that echoed around their small kitchen on Saturday afternoons? And Asha who taught yoga, took three sugars in her coffee and always brought tiny, oozing honey cakes to go with it? They never called round any more. No one did. Not even Mr Lavinski from next door, cup in hand, *to borrow a spot of milk till pension day*.

Daniel made people disappear.

And his stupid soup was spoiled before you opened the tin. Just like everything else he touched. But Billie needed to get to the kitchen and try to eat some anyway before Mam came looking for her again.

Back in the bedroom, and freed from his soggy towel, Bird took himself to the top of the wardrobe, where his sideways stare at Billie suggested he held her responsible for his damp, dishevelled state. As she dried and dressed, he shook and preened himself. His eyes grew narrow; heavy. Closed.

'That's it,' Billie whispered. 'You sleep then. I'll bring you back some food too,' she added. 'I'll find something. And whatever it is, it'll be much nicer that Daniel's soup.'

# SIXTEEN

Mam *had* made soup from scratch after all: thick orange butternut squash soup, with something spicy that lit tiny fires on Billie's tongue. Mam smiled at Billie as they sipped it from silvery spoons, blowing some of the heat away before it touched their lips. Her hair had curled at the front while she'd stirred the pan and her cheeks grew pink as she ate. She looked almost like old Mam. Almost. Even with Daniel away, her eyes still darted from clock to door and back again and she seemed somehow to hover on her chair as if she couldn't really commit to sitting for long.

'This is nice,' Billie said. 'Is it one of Dad's recipes?'

Mam shook her head. 'No, Billie,' she said. 'It's from a book.'

Billie stared into her soup, wishing she could find the words that she needed next at the bottom of it.

'Why *did* he stop writing, Mam?'

Mam's spoon stopped, suspended midway between her bowl and her mouth.

'I've no idea, Billie. You know that.'

'You're *sure* they'd tell us though, wouldn't they – the prison people – if Dad was sick? If . . . if . . . something was wrong?' Billie let soup trickle from her spoon, watched it fall; afraid to look at Mam. Afraid of the answer she might see in her face.

Mam put down her spoon. Sighed. Her hand rested on Billie's. Billie stared at it.

There were tiny cracks in the skin around the nails. It felt dry. Old Mam's hands were soft.

'He's not sick, Billie.'

Billie pushed her bowl away. The soup slopped up the sides of the bowl, a mini storm in an orange sea.

'How do you know?' she said, louder than she'd intended, like the storm was building inside her voice too.

'We've talked about this, Billie –'

'But Dad wouldn't just stop writing for no reason. He wouldn't. You *know* he wouldn't, Mam.'

Mam moved her hand. 'I didn't think he would break the law, Billie. But he did, didn't he?' She looked Billie in the eye. 'If your dad wanted to be in touch, he would. It's up to him. No good would come of chasing him about it.'

A sudden scatter of hail hit the window. Like someone was out there, throwing stones at the glass; trying to get their attention.

'But maybe he forgot our new address,' Billie said. 'I *said* we shouldn't move. What if he has? What if he can't find us? What if he thinks we moved away so he can't come home when he's ready? What if –'

'He knows where we are, Billie. He does. And there's Leon, remember? His probation officer. If there was a problem, if your dad *was* ill – any of that – well, he'd have let us know, wouldn't he?'

Leon. Beard. Braided hair. A voice that whispered like the wind but had steel in it. She'd forgotten about him. Tears pressed behind her eyes. Yes, he would have told them, wouldn't he? Unless . . .

'Does Leon know we've moved? Did you tell him?'

Mam nodded.

'Well, if Dad wouldn't want us to worry,' Billie insisted, 'he'd probably tell Leon not to say anything.'

Mam's hand was back. 'Prison can change people, Billie.' She shrugged. 'Maybe your dad wants a fresh start. Maybe he's . . . ashamed. I don't know. And I'm sorry. Sorry he did this to you. To all of us. But we have our new life too. You'll be OK. We all will.'

Billie whisked her hand from beneath Mam's. Threw down her spoon.

'No!' she shouted, suddenly clearer than ever. 'Dad wouldn't do that. You're only saying that because you want your precious Daniel instead of him. Well, I don't, OK? And I don't see why you do either. Daniel just wants to be in charge of you, he shouts at you, and he doesn't let you have any friends, and he isn't kind except when he's pretending because he's done something bad.'

Mam slid away from the table, gathered the bowls and cutlery, began rinsing them under a furious tap. She was hiding, trying not to cry, Billie knew. She moved closer, touched Mam's shoulder.

'Can we go there? To the prison? Just to make *sure* Dad's all right. *Please*, Mam.'

Mam's shoulders stiffened.

'That's enough now, Billie. I've said what I think ...'

'Have you though, Mam?' Billie shouted. Words tumbled out as if they'd been pressed back behind a locked door. 'Or have you said what Daniel thinks? Like you do about everything else. Well, he might be in charge of your whole life but he's not in charge of mine, and he's not in charge of me and my dad so he can't stop me from checking up on Dad and neither can you!'

She rushed from the kitchen with a door slam that rattled the pictures in the hall. She only remembered about Bird's dinner when she was back in her bedroom. Her fury ebbed as he stared up at her from multicoloured chaos on the floor. Her pot of felt-tip pens toppled and scattered. A snowstorm of shredded tissue. The belt from her dressing gown curled among it all like a giant red worm. Bird dipped his head. Something glinted green and silver in his beak: a sweet wrapper. He stepped through the muddle, picking up his feet as carefully as a ballet dancer, stopped by Billie's slippers.

'That for me?' She held out her hand, smiled. The fire in her head cooled a little. But Bird hopped away with his treasure, proceeded to tuck it under the corner of the bedside rug.

'Funny little thing,' Billie said. 'Part-raven, part-magpie, eh?'

Bird squawked, opened his throat wide, stared pointedly at Billie.

'Hungry after all your fun, aren't you?' Billie was cross with herself. She'd meant to break off some bread from the loaf they'd had with their soup; maybe sneak some rind from Daniel's precious bacon in the fridge while Mam was clearing up, some berries if Mam had bought any. She hadn't meant to have the Dad conversation again. It had pushed its way out of her head and into the room. And now *everything* felt worse.

'Can you wait just a bit longer, Bird?' she said. 'There's something I need to do first, something important. For my dad.'

She glanced at her alarm clock. With Daniel away, she was betting that Mam would soon settle in front of the TV, watch her soap. She might doze a bit, like she used to. Billie could sneak into her bedroom, borrow the laptop. She would Google the address and telephone number for the prison, have a look at the route, check for buses and things.

The more she thought about it, the more she knew something was wrong. Dad needed to reach her. And Bird – well, somehow, Bird had come to tell her that.

She watched as he tugged his sweet-wrapper treasure from its hiding place, held it in one foot and begin to nibble the edges. She smiled. Maybe he could still taste chocolate mint there. He definitely was hungry. While she had that laptop, she'd better do a quick search about ravens too, find out about a healthier diet for this very special messenger.

SEVENTEEN

Billie checked everywhere but the laptop was nowhere to be found. Drawers, bedside cupboard and wardrobe: full of nothing but clothes, underwear and socks, all folded into exact, regular shapes – even the socks. Like you saw in shops where they never put prices on things, but it didn't matter because most people couldn't afford them anyway; wouldn't dare touch them even if they could. Mam and Dad used to laugh together at those shops; dare one another to run in and mess up the displays then run out again.

The memory squeezed at her heart . . .

She was wasting her time. Daniel must have taken the laptop with him. She'd have to try with the school one. Unless . . .

Under the bed. Where Mam sometimes kept important things before Daniel moved in?

No. No laptop. Just a suitcase and a cardboard box full of the brightly coloured hats, jumpers and scarves Mam always wore in winter. Her *sunshine clothes*, she always said, now squashed together and grey with under-bed dust. Billie stared at them, thought of the Mam that had somehow been packed away with them. The Mam that had spent the last coins in her purse on every yellow sunflower in the corner shop, because Billie had been stuck indoors with scarlet fever for the sunniest week of the school holidays. The Mam that smiled under a wide summer sky, who made fabulous, fruity flapjacks but burned every piece of toast she ever made because she'd been dancing to the radio in the kitchen. Or chatting to a worried friend on the phone. The Mam whose laugh exploded like a firework in quiet rooms . . .

The ice splinter stabbed, cold and sharp in Billie's throat.

Dad had stolen some of Mam's colours along with the money he'd 'borrowed' from work. Billie knew that. But Daniel – Daniel was packing every last scrap of them away; squashing Mam; greying her out just like her forgotten sunshine hats and scarves.

Both her parents: missing. She should have done something sooner.

Well, there was no time to waste now . . .

Billie closed the cardboard flaps and pushed the box

out of sight, her whole body aching around the hole in her heart.

There was just the suitcase to check. The laptop wouldn't be in there, would it? It wasn't heavy enough.

The jangle of ad-break music rose and fell through the walls. Mam might nip out to put the kettle on. *Be quick, Billie.*

The catch on the case was rusted and stiff; didn't budge.

The lounge door squeaked open.

Mam. In the kitchen now.

Billie tucked the case under her arm. She'd investigate it in the safety of her own room and get it back before Mam's programme finished.

She had to use both hands to free the catch, snagged the edge of her thumb as she fought with it. As it snapped open, and Billie lifted the lid, Bird fluttered down beside her.

'Just stupid papers, Bird,' Billie said. 'After all that.'

There were bills – some with angry red print and addressed to Dad. And important-looking documents to do with the flat, some with a sort of crown stamped on the corner. Scribbled notes torn out of a pad that made no sense. Billie lifted a few from the top, let them fall back. There was only more of the same underneath. What a

159

waste of time. She sighed. What now?

Bird's head jerked to one side. His black bead eye brightened. He hopped closer to the case, then fluttered up on to one edge and began pecking at the papers with his hooked beak.

Probably spotted a paperclip or something else bright, Billie thought.

No. A key, attached to a grubby piece of string. The key to the garage block! Billie had been wondering where that had gone. She tugged it free.

'Come on, Bird,' she said, holding out her arm for him to step on to. '*I* need that key. And you're a raven, not a magpie. Mam'll think we've got mice if you peck holes in her papers . . .'

Then she saw it. A corner of an envelope.

Tissue-thin.

Blue.

Her heart raced. Thin blue paper. Blue like Dad's letters on the mat.

Prison blue.

She pulled it free, watched it tremble in her hand. The bold capitals: HMP HELMSFIELD stared up at her. Next to it, a date stamp. Faded ink. Billie squinted at the numbers. June. It was stamped in June. This year . . . six months after Dad's last letter. There was a rough, jagged tear across the top, like someone had opened it in a hurry.

Billie's heart thudded. Her fingers shook.

Was this it? The bad-news letter? Had Mam kept it from her?

She felt inside. Same tissue-thin paper as before. Two folded sheets. She eased them out, glimpsed black lettering through the almost transparent, lined sheets. Could something so flimsy, so delicate, bring heavy, horrible news? Could it?

She unfolded it, Mam and the ad break forgotten. There was nothing but Billie and the blue bird letter, poised in her hand, wings spread wide.

Her eyes blurred. But she knew. Spidery writing that sloped across the page, ran to the edges like it couldn't be contained there. Wild writing.

Dad's writing.

Dad's letter. To Mam.

Billie's thoughts whirled. Her heart hammered.

The words jumped around, wouldn't stay still or make sense. In another world, wind pushed at the window, rain ran in crazy rivers down the glass. A door creaked. TV music swelled.

Billie squeezed her eyes closed. Opened them. Focused

through tears. Her heartbeat grew faster and louder as she read . . .

Dad said he was coming out; said he knew he couldn't come home right away . . . That Mam would need time . . . maybe they could talk.

Leon had found him work – farm work. That was good news. And it wasn't too far from his mam's old place, he thought. He'd write with an address soon. Leon was helping.

But Billie. Tell my Billie I'll be over to see her the minute I'm free. September time. September stars. Before the whooper swans fly south for winter . . .

Billie's thoughts whirled. What was this? How come she didn't know about it? How come Mam hadn't said anything?

She held the letter closer to the light, checked the date. Yes. June. He wrote it in June. This year! Now it was November. Nearly December, the swans long settled in warmer waters, sailing on warmer air. But still no Dad. Why hadn't he come? Surely he would have tried? Her throat tightened.

Had he come to the flat and been sent away? By Mam? By Daniel?

Had Mam replied to this letter? She hadn't even mentioned it to Billie. She'd even suggested that Dad had forgotten about her. Had moved on without her . . .

Who *was* this new Mam?

Billie stared at the mess of papers where Bird was nestled ready for a nap. What else was it hiding? She lifted Bird clear. He gave a small squawk of protest and scuttled under her bed where he watched Billie through narrowed eyes from under the edge of the duvet.

'Sorry, Bird,' Billie whispered. She tipped the case upside down, scattered the mess of white, red, black ink with frantic fingers; scanned for prison blue.

There. Crumpled as if someone had scrunched it into a ball then smoothed it out again – another letter.

Her fingers tensed as she read, almost pressed holes in the tissue-thin paper.

Dad had given an address, as he'd promised. But the ink was smudged . . .

Something *Farm. Malham* . . . was it? . . . Dale? *Route from Skipton, remember?*

Billie couldn't make it out.

Something, something . . . *Malham Cove. Tell Billie peregrine falcons nest there in summer* . . .

Skipton. A busy little market town with leaning

163

medieval houses and tea rooms with small, wonky windows. Billie had been there once. On a school trip to Knaresborough with its petrifying well where hats, pots and pans, and teddy bears hung, stilled forever; turned to stone. They'd been to an abbey too, partly in ruins – had eaten lunch there, while swallows dived through ruined archways that led only to more sky. Bolton Abbey. That was it.

Her heart soared like the swallows: the Skipton area. Malham. What was that? A village? A town? It couldn't be too hard to reach. There'd be buses, trains if it was near Skipton. And there were the other clues: Malham Cove. The peregrine falcons. They were rare, hard to find. If there were peregrine falcon nests, Dad would be close by. She'd find him. Everybody knew everybody in the Dales, he always said. Someone would know Dad. She'd go there, to Malham – and the cove. She'd ask around . . .

But the address – Malham, or whatever – it was *only temporary.*

Billie's heart made small leaps, like there was a bird inside her chest, battering against her ribs, trying to find a way out. *How* temporary? This letter was dated August 11th – would he have moved by now?

Had she missed him? Coldness crept over her, like she might be turning to stone too.

She read on. Dad's writing was smaller here, tighter somehow: the letters squished one against the other, hard to untangle. His words seemed to struggle stop-start across the page, as if he didn't really want to write them. Sad words that hid lots of others that weren't there. Billie could *feel* them.

He thanked Mam for writing back . . .

He was upset, but he understood why Billie was angry. Hurt. He knew Mam was trying to do what she thought best for Billie.

He'd let them down. He knew that . . .

He missed them both.

He hoped . . .

He knew he had no right.

Bolder words now, just above his name at the bottom of the page.

Just, please — tell Billie I'm here when she's ready.
Here under the Dales stars, waiting for her to find her
way back home to me like the spring swans. Or the
summer falcons . . .

A second blue sheet. On it, a sketch of a bird, carefully coloured in with crayon. A black bearded bird with dinosaur claws and petrol-in-a-puddle colours on its wings.

A raven.

Dad's black crayon had pierced the fragile paper, left a small hole in the bird's wedge-shaped tail.

Bird waddled out from under the bed, stretched his neck forward, pecked at the edge of the drawing.

Billie dragged her sleeve across her eyes, sniffed.

'I know, Bird,' she said. 'Dad's drawn *you*.'

EIGHTEEN

Billie felt crushed and crumpled; as tissue thin as Dad's letter. He'd wanted to see her. Mam hadn't let him come. She'd told him Billie was angry with him when all she wanted was to be with him again. She *did* have questions. She *had* been angry – sometimes she still was. It didn't matter. This was *Dad*. Mam *knew* that.

Why had she kept all this from Billie? How *dare* she . . .?

Billie's jaw clenched. Fire flashed in her head. This must have been Daniel's idea. Mam couldn't be so cruel, could she? No. Not even *new* Mam could. Daniel must have made her.

She folded Dad's letters carefully into her dressing-gown pocket, as gently as if they were living creatures. She scooped up the contents of the suitcase, threw them back inside. The lid dropped like a metal-edged jaw. Her fists tightened. Her blood thundered. She was having this out with Mam – *now*.

167

Bird hopped towards her, head tilted, as if unsure about this red-faced, angry Billie. She was scaring him. She took a slow breath, let her racing blood slow a little.

'It's OK,' she said. 'Come here, Bird.' She held out her arm, felt his feet close around it. Felt the joining of things again. The connecting. She thought of Dad's careful drawing. The message in it. The love in it. Her blood slowed a little. Nothing could break the connection between the two of them, could it? Not prison. Not time. Not lies or stolen letters.

But what if he *did* think she didn't love him any more? What if he *had* moved on now – pushed her from his mind because remembering her hurt too much. Like when she'd pushed his box of things out of sight, high on the top of her wardrobe? Her heart stung as if his sharp black crayon had pierced that too.

But . . . he had drawn that raven. And a *raven* had come to her. Had come *for* her . . .

This was a sign. A bird message, speaking to Billie as clearly as those weather messages painted in the sky.

Well, she had an address now. So she – and Bird – were going to the Dales to find Dad and tell him everything. She just needed to figure out how.

Mam's voice now, from somewhere far away . . .

Billie jumped; froze. Was she calling her? Coming this way?

The voice moved. A door closed. The voice grew muffled. No. Mam was on the phone.

No prizes for guessing who she was talking to. Billie placed her hand over her pocket, cradled the letters through the bobbled fabric of her dressing gown. She couldn't confront Mam. What had she been *thinking*? Mam had lied, hidden Dad's letters in her case. She couldn't know Billie had found them, found Dad's address. She'd know exactly what Billie would do and she'd try to stop her. Worse, she'd tell Daniel. She'd be scared not to; scared of the splinter-thin moments that would follow if he found out she'd hidden it from him.

How had she not understood before now? Mam was frightened of Daniel. Every bit as frightened as Billie was.

No. She couldn't say anything at all. She just had to go. Once she got to Dad, he'd know what to do. How to get Mam away from Daniel. How to set them all free . . .

Daniel would be back from his trip on Friday. Billie needed to travel to the Dales before then. Her worry worms nibbled at her insides. No. Running away would only stir things up – cause trouble for Mam. She would call the police, wouldn't she? Daniel would *not* like that.

She needed to be there and *back* before he returned. Back with Dad. Before the storm-threat in Daniel released its full fury with Mam in its path. Together, Billie and Dad would make sure Mam was safe. And the secrets would be out, anyway. No one would be able to pretend any more.

Billie wouldn't have to pretend any more.

She wouldn't have to live with Daniel. There'd be no more ice-splinter silences and no risk of being stolen away to live with strangers. She'd have her dad.

If only she had a phone, like everyone else in her class, maybe it would give her the quickest route – on Google maps. Never mind. There was always the library computer. She could look up bus timetables, trains to this Malham-whatever-it-was. And wait: Dad's maps, his old compass, books about the Dales – they'd be in those boxes Daniel shoved in the garage, wouldn't they? And Billie had the key. She fished it from her pocket, watched it swing back and forth on its grey string, like a pendulum, ticking away the seconds. Bird watched it too, mesmerised by the movement.

How many seconds until Friday? Best not waste any. She'd make some excuse and investigate the garage that evening.

The rain had other ideas, turned to icy sleet that sliced sideways though the air for the rest of the day. There'd be a row if Billie insisted on going out in this. Especially on a school night. Even Bird had turned his back to the window after his late supper of bacon rind, breadcrumbs, and a large dead spider he'd found in a corner of the room. He hunkered down on Billie's bed and fluffed out his feathers. He might enjoy a warm shower, but he felt differently about this kind of soaking. He was going nowhere.

Luckily, Mam had chores to do, and work she'd fallen behind on for the next day. She wanted to say that if Mam stopped doing so much cleaning, she wouldn't be behind with work and she could relax. But she kept quiet. She couldn't face another one of Mam's nice film and popcorn sessions. It wouldn't be just the two of them this time. There'd be a huge elephant with sharp tusks wedged between them. Mam would know it was there and Billie would have to pretend it wasn't. She wasn't sure she could.

She lay down beside Bird with paper and pencil and started two lists ready for the next day: things to do, and things she needed to find. Things for Bird. Bird watched the pencil move through sleep-squinty eyes, made a small pecking gesture each time it came anywhere near him.

Billie shifted further away. 'Go to sleep, Bird,' she said. 'I need to concentrate.'

She thought hard, chewed the end of the pencil. Her worry worms chewed *her*. There were so many things to sort out. Could she really do this, all by herself? She didn't know where she was going, not really; couldn't remember anything about the route or how far it was to Skipton, let alone on to Malham Cove. Would it be one bus journey or more? Would there even be a bus and what would the fare be? If she didn't have enough, was it the sort of terrain you could cover on foot – in winter? No matter how hard she tried, Billie only clearly remembered two things about the actual journey to and from the Dales on that school trip. One was when the mint choc chip ice cream she'd spent all her trip money on toppled from the cone and spattered on to the tarmac in the bus park: blue-green and speckled like a fallen blackbird's egg. The other thing was that Orla McCabe made up a 'sad' song about it and sang it all the way home on the coach.

What if she did manage the journey; found Dad's address, but Dad wasn't there? She'd have no more money. She wouldn't have any food . . .

She wouldn't even be able to get back home.

And anyway, if she went off like this, Mam would be terrified. She'd definitely call the police then, wouldn't she? Daniel would be livid.

Once, Mr Lavinski had called the police, worried, he'd said, about raised voices and thumps and thuds from the flat next door. Billie's flat.

Daniel had told them lies, of course. Blamed the TV. And Mam had backed him up. But Daniel had stormed and fumed for a week. Billie had seen Daniel leaning into Mr Lavinski's open doorway. And Mr Lavinski never came to borrow milk or sugar again after that.

If Billie got this wrong, if she didn't make it back in time – with Dad – she'd have made everything *ten* times worse . . .

The wind heaved another handful of hail at her window; whistled through Mam's makeshift repair and lifted goosebumps on Billie's arms. Even Bird shivered under his feathered clothes. It was cold enough for more snow just like the forecast had said. Snow was the last thing Billie needed for her journey. Snow could block roads, cancel buses and trains, close schools and shops. Worse, Dad said he'd be living on a farm, not far from Nan's old place. That was miles from the nearest village, she was sure, with only sheep for neighbours. When Dad was growing up, he and his mam got cut off for weeks in winter. Word pictures of his childhood floated into her mind . . .

Dales snow, Billie: that's different from town snow. Sudden. Silent. Pure, diamond-white, and perfect, covering hills, valleys, rooftops, roads, rail tracks, everything – like someone threw a great cloth down overnight. Stunning, but a force to be reckoned with. It freezes waterfalls. Flings ice-daggers on to rooftops and bridges. Sweeps away pathways and roads. Turns soil to stone, steals food from the animals and birds and seals it underground. Takes your breath away, it does. About as beautiful as it gets. But you don't mess with it, Billie-Blue. Folk that live there, they know: Dales snow – you have to be ready for it. If you're not, it can snuff out your life like a sword.

Billie looked at her pathetic list of provisions, thought of her thin winter coat; her last winter's boots that had no room for extra socks any more; imagined Bird, desperately pecking at frozen ground; starving hungry and huddling against her for warmth she couldn't give him. Of Dad, finding them both too late – frozen stone-cold solid like the petrified stuffed animals in the Knaresborough cave. She shivered, pulled up the hood of her dressing gown. Felt herself shrink down inside its purple softness, mouse-small and scared.

Purple. A memory stirred . . .

A purple flower. So tiny it might blow away with the wind, yet it lived and thrived in the Arctic; weathered the biting gales and mountainous snowdrifts; the merciless ice. Dad had shown it to her in a book. What was it called? She pressed hard at the memory; saw Dad's finger, stained green from the garden, moving across a glossy page: *'Purple saxifrage,'* he read. *'The hardiest plant in the world. Occurring in the Arctic, Alps, Rocky Mountains, and some parts of Northern Britain, including the Yorkshire Dales. Solitary purple flowers on short stalks. Fragile plants that survive by clustering together close to the ground, giving one another shelter and support against the harshest conditions on this earth . . .'*

Dad's eyes, gentle on hers. *'See, Billie-Blue. See?'*

She sat up a little taller. She could do it. She had Bird. Bird had her. And Dad was there, just like he'd said, with her even while he was away, making her strong. And maybe, just maybe, there'd be others to help her along the way . . . if she was brave enough to ask.

'Purple saxifrage, Bird,' she said. 'That's what we'll be.'

She blew out a long breath.

'But *still,*' Billie whispered into the freezing air. *'Please* don't let there be snow on the Dales . . .'

She hid her half-finished lists under her pillow and dozed fitfully. She dreamed of black birds painted on grey prison walls, Dad's voice drifting on a wild winter wind, and her name – Billie-Blue – scribbled in purple letters across a snow-laden sky.

NINETEEN

Billie ran all the way home after school, library book and printed sheets bouncing against her back. She raced to change out of her uniform before heading for the garage. She couldn't risk tell-tale dust on the navy fabric; didn't want Mam asking questions, getting wind that she might be up to something. And anyway, she wasn't allowed in the garage, messing with Daniel's things in there. Another of his stupid rules. She cleared up Bird's latest bedroom chaos, scraped bird mess from the floor.

'If only you could use the loo as well as the shower, Bird,' she said. For once, she was glad to have no carpet. It made things easier. Bird lifted his feathers in something very like a shrug and fluttered on to Billie's shoulder, nibbled strands of hair that had freed themselves from her hairband.

One eye on the kitchen clock – just like Mam – she set the table and peeled potatoes at record speed. Bird perched beside her, catching peel as it curled from her knife. He tossed each piece on to the floor in disdain, as if disappointed by a new species of flat, tasteless, worm. Another cleaning-up job for Billie. She hunted around the fridge, found the last of the bacon at the back. That would keep him happy for a bit. Mam was going to notice the disappearing bacon issue: Billie would have to say it was out of date, so she'd thrown it away. No way was she saying she'd eaten it herself. After tea, she'd go to the corner shop – say she needed stuff for cookery class tomorrow. Which was true. Sort of. She had Mrs Scrivens's recipe for apple cinnamon crumble in her bag. She wouldn't be making any, but Mam wasn't to know. She'd put the cookery money with her birthday savings – use it to buy tickets for her trip and drinks and things on her way. She'd see what she could find for Bird too – although hopefully he would find things for himself, like he'd started to do that day in Tanglewood. Her worry worms were back, tumbling and twisting; making her feel sick. Was this stealing – like Dad? It was dishonest, she knew that. Hated it. But it was for a good cause. The best. Not just for herself, but for the people she loved most in the world. For her family. She gulped past a new lump in her throat. That *was* the same as Dad.

Cookery money wasn't very much, though. Did that

make it better? She sighed. It didn't, she knew. She'd find a way to pay it back. And Mam would understand once she was safe.

The worry worms didn't give up. If there was a bus, how much would the fare cost? What if she needed a train? She'd never afford that. How much food would she need? A day's worth? Two?

She'd just have to get by. '*Purple saxifrage*,' she whispered to herself. She'd think of something. She had to.

Bird swallowed the last of the bacon and flew to the top of the fridge; began stabbing at the door with his hooked beak. Billie smiled.

'Nothing more in there for you, Bird. C'mon. Let's get to the garage. You can feast on spiders and flies and keep out of trouble for a bit while I'm finding Dad's things.'

He fluttered down on to her shoulder. Billie held open her backpack, dangled a saved strip of bacon rind above it, made it wriggle like a live worm. 'In you go, Bird,' she said.

Bird considered the black depths of the bag, head on one side. Squawked. Was he going to be difficult? No. The bacon lure worked. But he screeched so loudly that Billie had to cover her ears when she tried to zip the bag shut. He'd have to get used to the bag, though – travelling all the way to the Dales with a raven on her shoulder, or even under her coat, wasn't exactly practical; would draw far too much attention.

She made her way sneak-soft down the stairwell and across the yard with a grey beak poking out over the edge; one liquorice eye clockwork-blinking under the lights. Thankfully, no one was about except Mr Lavinski putting something in the bins. And he didn't have his glasses on.

The garage door was stiff and heavy. It groaned like a disgruntled beast as Billie heaved it upwards; stuck about a metre from the ground. She had to crawl underneath, bird and backpack clutched against her chest with one arm. She straightened up, waited for her eyes to adjust. It was already dark outside and little light crept in under the door or through the tiny window, which was blinded by years of dirt.

There was a light, Billie remembered, a long cord switch to pull somewhere to the right of the door. But that might draw attention. She'd best use her torch. She set down her bag, stifled a sneeze in the dust-thick air. Bird scrabbled, unperturbed by darkness or dust, drawn, no doubt, by scuttling sounds from behind the boxes and shrouded shapes stacked around the walls. Either very large spiders or mice, Billie thought. Ravens would eat both, according to her online search.

'Sorry, mice,' she whispered. 'It's just the way of things . . .'

Her torch flared yellow, glanced off the red reflector bulb and silver frame of a bike. Dad's bike. It was propped against a tea chest, one wheel turned outwards and pedals frozen mid-spin, as if Dad had been snatched from the saddle and the bike was waiting for him to resume his ride. Billie ran a hand over the handlebars. They were cold, strung with thick, intricate webs that clung to Billie's fingers as she moved away like grimy netting. The chain looked rusty in the torchlight; dangling in a loop at one side. Billie's throat tightened. Dad loved that bike. Once he was home, she'd help him clean and polish it, grease the gears and oil the chain, have the wheels spinning free, flashing diamonds, just like before. And the spiders, they could move somewhere new.

Dad's things were easy to find, the boxes shoved together against the back wall, as if Daniel wanted them as far away from the door as possible. Already, they were grey with dust. Dead flies lay scattered across the top.

Just clothes in the first two. A careless tangle of shirts, jeans, jumpers, and shoes. Billie stared at them in the half-light. A single burning tear ran down her nose, landed among them. It was like looking at pieces of Dad, discarded;

crammed together like they were nothing. Like he was nothing. She lifted the arm of his Guernsey sweater. His favourite.

Made for the outdoors, Billie, like me. Like you . . .

No woody smell of Dad any more. Just dust and must and a small hole eaten away by moths.

More of the same in the second box. Dad's weathered brown boots thrown in among the clothes; ridged soles caked with mud, now dry and grey as old plaster. A shrivelled oak leaf clung to one of them. A tiny brindle feather floated from the other as she picked it up.

The hole in Billie's heart grew wider. Her throat felt thick, her mouth dry, like the dust and mud was in there too, clogging it; making it harder to breathe . . .

She bit down on her lip. *Come on, Billie*, she thought. *Dad's back out there now, out with the winter leaves and winter birds. There'll be Dales mud on his boots, wide skies above him.*

Soon, she'd be there with him. She *would*.

The third box was a treasure trove. Dad's explorers' backpack, roomier than Billie's school bag was quickly filled with maps, a flask and water bottle . . . Dad's waterproofs, jacket and hat – too big, but *the right gear, the right equipment, for the wilds, Billie, that's what it's all about*

– his *Book of British Birds* sat on the top; thumbed pages, a dark stain on the cover where Billie had spilled hot chocolate in her excitement at seeing her first owl. She could still see it now, swift, silent and secret; eyes like yellow fire in the night . . .

But where was Dad's compass? Billie needed that. Even if she couldn't remember exactly how to read it, having that around her neck felt important, as if somehow Dad would be there resting against her heart as she journeyed.

Bird emerged from his foraging; wings draped with stringy shreds of cobweb, which he didn't seem to notice. Quick-snap, his beady magpie eye caught a glimmer as Billie rummaged among more books, magazines, odd gloves, pencils, and pint-pots. He landed on top of them. There was a tap-click of beak on metal.

The compass.

'Clever, clever Bird,' Billie said. 'Thank you.'

It fitted in the palm of her hand, smooth and round like a golden pebble. Billie turned it over, squinted at the letters there, traced them with a fingernail. Too small to read in the gloom, but Billie knew what they said.

For wild wanderings.
And to bring you home.

Billie's heart clenched. Could Mam feel that way about Dad again? She didn't know . . .

But *home*. Home was Billie and Dad, together. It didn't matter where. Home was Mam being Mam. Home was feeling safe.

Billie needed to bring them all home . . .

She'd best finish up, get back and switch on the dinner before Mam arrived. Make everything seem normal. She covered her tracks, setting the boxes back where she'd found them, re-sticking Daniel's stupid tape as best she could. Bird jumped happily into her bag this time – either he was tired, or he'd spotted an escapee spider in there.

She gave Dad's bike a last look and flicked off her torch.

The sudden darkness split yellow – two great beams: searchlights reaching under the partly open door. The roar and splutter of a car engine, the swish-crunch of tyres on the wet concrete yard outside. A smell, deep and pungent in Billie's nostrils. Exhaust fumes. The sounds, the smell – all familiar . . .

Daniel's car with the hole in the exhaust that he was too mean to get fixed, even though it was polluting the entire world . . .

But it *couldn't* be.

The slam of a car door. Footsteps, quick, determined.

The grind of the garage door, pushed high on its rusty hinges. The click-swing of the pull cord. Blinding white light.

It *was*. Daniel. Commando hat. Red face; eyes glaring.

'Billie!' he said, his voice slither-soft, like a snake sliding through grass. 'What the – I've got important stuff in here! Who let you . . .? Out. Now.' His eyes, stone cold.

The twitch of his cheek.

His mouth, still moving. Angry shapes. The sounds, the words lost in a pandemonium of wingbeats and panicked squawks. Bird's black body ricocheting off the walls, beating against the tiny window. A swoop and snatch of claws. The crash-clatter of Dad's bike, toppled. On to Daniel's foot. A furious roar. The swipe-snatch of his fists in the air.

'Leave him! Stop it!' Billie yelled, snatching at Daniel's jacket. 'You're scaring him.'

Bird swooped low, claws heading straight for Daniel's head. He stooped, shouted; his face, his fists – murderous now. Reaching. Grabbing for a weapon, finding Dad's old garden spade.

'Go, Bird, go!' Billie shouted. 'Go. Get away!'

Bird swooped towards the gaping mouth of the garage, hovered for a second on the air, eyes glinting, fixed on Billie's own. In that second, the swing of metal in the air.

Bird, tumbling in the air like a ball.

Bird. Still on the concrete floor. The strobes of silver, sleety rain bouncing through the open door.

Billie stared at Daniel. He'd killed him. He'd killed Bird.

Silence yawned like a tear in time. A scream sounded inside her head. But Billie knew that she was silent. She felt herself shrink small; curl up tight inside herself. She hunkered down, shivered, just like Bird behind his hopeless tree. She stared at Daniel's shiny brown brogues and tried not to be there at all.

'Up,' Daniel hissed. 'Out.'

He pushed at Bird with his boot, moved him out into the yard. 'Hopefully a cat'll take it,' he grunted. 'Save me a job.'

He shoved Billie forward. She stared at Bird, limp and still under the bounce of silver, sleety rain. Hated herself for letting it happen.

For not having kept him safe.

For having no voice at all.

TWENTY

Daniel was back because he was sick – flu, he was sure, not that anyone would care. And now this. Billie out of control, rifling through the garage where she knew she shouldn't be, and worse – she'd been keeping some filthy wild bird. Well, he'd dealt with that, like he had to deal with everything round here. It was gone. No good Billie whining or blaming him. She knew the rule about the garage. She knew how he felt about birds. Well, she'd learned her lesson good and proper. She'd do as she was told from now on, maybe.

She'd had that thing in her bedroom too. What was Mam doing, letting it happen? Had she seen the state of Billie's floor? How long had the thing been in the house? That would be what had made him ill. Mam must've known. She knew how he felt about birds. About cleanliness. About kids knowing their place. Well, it went to prove it. He was right all along. She was hopeless and Billie was trouble, just like her dad . . .

On and on and on he went, finger stabbing the air in

the kitchen, while a pan of boiling eggs burned dry on a scarlet cooker plate, and no one moved to rescue them.

Then silence, louder than a train.

Billie's chest felt empty. Hollow. Like her heart had been knocked from her chest, was out there, lying in the rain with Bird.

Words whirled and flapped around her head; words to sting and stop Daniel in his tracks. He was evil. A murderer. She hated him. She'd report him. She hated Mam for bringing him here.

It was *her* garage, her dad's things in there. It was none of his business. Bird had been *her* secret. Mam hadn't known. Anyway, this was their flat: they could have a billion birds there if they wanted. Daniel was the one that didn't belong. The one making people ill. Bird had been beautiful. Special. Her friend. Her dad was beautiful too. She was glad if she was like him . . .

But her mouth was frozen shut, criss-cross-taped like the garage boxes. Unspoken words settled like boulders in her chest, in her throat. A roadblock.

Mam was saying something now. What was it? Billie's ears were full of dust.

Mam's hand on Daniel's arm. He shook it off; swatted it away like a fly and stormed out of the room.

Mam's eyes, wide as lakes. The pan hissing. The angry red hob. An explosion – egg debris on the stovetop; on the lino by Mam's feet.

Mam's hand flew to her mouth. She looked as horrified as Billie. For a moment, Billie wanted to reach for her, be scooped into her arms; wanted to leave the kitchen with its sulphur stench and thick air. Leave the flat. Leave their life with Daniel. Together.

She didn't. Couldn't.

She'd brought Daniel. Let him hurt Billie. Let him kill Bird.

A chasm wider than the sky stretched between Billie and Mam now. Four words loosened, threatened to fall into the space.

You hid Dad's letters.

Their sharp edges stung. But she couldn't let them out right now. Couldn't demand the answers she longed for. Couldn't let on that she knew. Mam would guess that she'd run to find Dad; keep a watch on her. Worse, Daniel was still simmering, ready to explode again like the forgotten eggs on the stove. Next time, it might be Billie or Mam that felt the full swing of his fury.

The air was shell-thin. So was Mam. However much Billie hated her right now, she needed to get to Dad more than ever; now. For both their sakes. She bent down, began collecting the shards of shell and sticky clumps of egg from the floor.

'We'll need the mop and bucket, Billie,' Mam whispered.

Billie nodded. When she fetched it from the cupboard, she took Dad's backpack from under the table and wedged it right at the back, behind the hoover. Luckily, no one had noticed that she'd carried it in, rather than her own school bag. That sat abandoned in the garage, a home for spiders.

Later, as she lay in her room with a single dark feather in her hand, the tears came. Her beautiful Bird – her special friend, her messenger from Dad – was gone. Dead. And in the end, it was because of her. She'd brought him to danger, let him down in the worst way. She'd let Dad down too.

Her heart ached for him, left out there in the rain like piece of rag. Left out for the cats to take. She couldn't bear it. She felt sick. Longed to go to him, wrap him up and give him a proper burial. A proper goodbye. But there was no way she could escape the flat. Not tonight.

Voices sounded like close-range ammunition above the sound of the television. Daniel. Mam. Daniel . . . Daniel . . . Daniel. Come the morning, there'd be repercussions for her 'behaviour'. She'd be lucky if Daniel let her out of her room to go to school. She didn't care. Not really. Except that she needed to find Dad. Needed him to know that she hadn't abandoned him. That she hadn't known about his letters. That she loved him.

Needed him to help her make sure that Daniel never got to hurt anyone again.

She was going to find him. Even though now – somehow – she would have to go alone. Without Bird. She'd let Bird down. Now she had to do whatever it took to put everything else right.

She held the soft black feather under her chin, covered her ears and pictured a solitary purple flower, head held high against the howl of an Arctic wind. She squeezed her eyes tighter and tighter until all she could see behind the lids was purple.

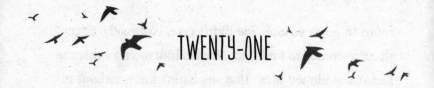

TWENTY-ONE

Billie did go to school the next day. Daniel said he had better things to do than childminding her and she didn't get to miss school for bad behaviour. But it was *straight home by 4 p.m.*, he said. *Not a second later*. And then she'd be *scrubbing out that bedroom from top to bottom*. She was grounded too, *make no mistake*. Maybe forever. Daniel didn't say. Neither did Mam. She just fiddled with her hair; kept swallowing, like she might have a roadblock building in her throat too, and handed Billie the bread and cheese for her lunchtime sandwiches.

Billie thought suddenly of Nell, shielding Bird against the stick kids, small, soaked through. Fierce. She had been afraid. But she had stood up for Bird anyway. Mam never tried to stand up for Billie.

Not even today . . . after what Daniel had done. She never even mentioned Bird.

But Billie hadn't protected Bird.

She and Mam. They were the same now.

The word boulders were still there in Billie's throat too. She kept her lips tightly closed to hold them in, even when Lola called her Ginger-frizz and tugged at her curls during class. Even when Alina, her favourite TA with the parrot-patterned shirt sat next to her by the library window, offered to let her have first choice of the new book delivery. Billie managed a shake of her head, but felt the boulders move, just a little. She had to look away and hide her eyes so Alina wouldn't read the stories there. Like Mrs Scriven might have done when Billie told her she'd left her cookery basket in the car; that she and Mam had picked apples together specially too . . .

Alina had smiled at her; said she was always here if anything was worrying Billie, that it helped to talk about things. When she got back to her desk, she'd written something on a notepad and underlined it with two sweeps of her pen.

On the walk back to class, Billie still searched the sky for Bird even though she knew he would not, could not be there. The hole in her heart spread wider, deepened like the clouds overhead. Even if she found Dad, she'd never see Bird again. Her throat ached around the word roadblock.

A raucous cry rang out above the hubbub of voices

and skip-scuffle of shoes on tarmac. Billie stopped in her tracks.

Bird?

Jamie Lawson bumped into her back, accidentally on purpose, she was sure. Her lunchbox fell to the floor and flipped open, threw her uneaten sandwich and green apple on to the floor. The cry came again – closer. Shannon's face loomed at her, mouth agape, arms flapping like wings.

'Hey, bird-girl. Gotcha!' She kicked Billie's apple, screamed with laughter as it hit the wall opposite. 'Goal,' she yelled and flapped away towards the rain shelter where her giggling gang cheered her on.

Billie's word boulders shifted, ready to fly through the air and knock Shannon from her feet. Just like Daniel might do. But she had to keep her head down. Bide her time. She couldn't draw attention to herself. Couldn't risk unblocking the words in her throat, or they'd all come tumbling out at once. Teachers would want to talk to Mam; worry about Billie's safety . . . start making plans of their own.

Nothing could get in the way of Billie finding Dad.

She waited until the playground was empty except for Mr Lau waving at her to *hurry up and come in now*. She stooped, collected up her spilled lunch. As she straightened: a flash of movement above the library roof, a black streak across the sky. Then nothing but empty air.

Billie waited as long as she dared for the playground to clear at home time, Daniel's curfew burning in her brain. She'd have to run most of the way home, but at least she'd be left to herself.

A duffle-coated girl – Nell – swung back and forth on the metal gate of the schoolyard. She jumped down when she spotted Billie; began her excited bird hops.

'I seen him again, I did,' she said, whispering this time, even though there was no one around to hear. 'Bird. On the roof of the bike sheds. Did you let 'im go? I thought you was keepin' him an' –'

Hope surged through Billie. Had she been wrong about Bird? There'd been no sign of his small black body that morning. *Could* he have survived after all? Just been stunned or something?

'What? When, Nell? When did you see him?' Billie grabbed Nell's arm. 'Where? Can you show me?'

Nell shook her head. A rainbow hair clip flew from her fringe, skidded across the playground. She ran to retrieve it, ran back to Billie. 'Just now,' she said. 'Kids were shouting at 'im and messing about. Swooped down over them he did – wings like a great big black bomber from Nan's war films. Right over their heads. Scared 'em stiff and they ran off. Serves them right, don't it, Billie?'

Billie chewed at her bottom lip. Scanned the sky. Remembered the slice-swing of the spade. Felt it slam against her heart. Remembered the still, crumpled feather bundle in the rain. What was she thinking? Bird was dead. She'd seen that with her own eyes. It wasn't Bird Nell had seen. It couldn't be.

Nell was tugging at her sleeve. 'Shall we go and find 'im, Billie?'

Billie took a deep breath. It shuddered in her chest. She couldn't do it. Couldn't tell Nell the truth about Bird. It was too awful. It was her fault. And if Nell knew about Bird, she'd know about Daniel. Billie was pretty sure that was a secret she wouldn't be able to keep from her nan.

Billie would have to tell a lie. She offered one with some truth inside it. Because Nell was probably her friend.

She rested her hand on Nell's, stilled it. 'No, Nell,' she said, her words squeezing past the roadblock boulders in her throat, making her voice sound scratchy; full of gravel. 'If we do see Bird again, we've got to ignore him this time, OK? He's a wild bird now. He's got to know that he is. He's got to keep away from people. Otherwise the other birds won't accept him. They might even kill him. My dad taught me that.'

Nell's eyes grew rounder than ever. She nodded, dislodging the clip that she had just pinned back in her wayward fringe. 'Kids might hurt him, an' all,' she whispered. She sighed. Her thin shoulders sank. 'So, you did let him go then?' she said.

Billie looked away, hid the tremble of her mouth. The boulders shifted closer together, blocking the truth behind them.

'Sort of.' She lifted her hood against the whip of the wind, hid her tell-tale eyes. 'I've got to go now,' she said. 'I've got to be home early.' She turned, set off. Stopped. 'Walk with me if you want,' she called. 'Long as you can walk *fast*.'

Nell's solemn expression changed as if the wind had whisked it away; replaced it with a snatch of sunshine. She gave a small skip, caught up with Billie.

'I got to be home quick, an' all,' she said. More bird hops from foot to foot. Her eyes glittered. 'Gotta help me nan get Florence ready. An' do some baking.' She paused, skipped again to keep pace with Billie. Beamed up at her. 'For Grassington. You goin' too? We always go. Nan, she –'

Billie stopped. Grassington.

There was a photo, tacked skew-whiff into an album – people in strange costumes – bonnets and the drape of shawls. Coloured lights. A tree. The memory floated, half-formed as if slowly developing in the old darkroom photo trays she'd seen on TV shows.

Dad had shown her. In his mam's old album. She'd taken him there when he was young. A fair. A festival or something . . .

Grassington was in the Dales. *Not far from my mam's old place.*

Not far from Malham then?

'You're going to Grassington? When? Why?'

Nell stared up at her, brow scrunched in disbelief. 'You *know*,' she said. '*Everyone* round here knows! The Victorian Christmas Fair! On Saturday.' She twirled her hair around one finger, hop-skipped higher than ever. 'Me nan's been every year since she were a nipper; never missed it, even when she were expecting me mam and she were as big as a house on wheels.' She stretched her arms wide, grinned her gappy grin.

Saturday. Just three days away. Billie's mind whirled. Could this be the answer? Could she wait until then?

They'd reached the play park. The swing-frame and slide loomed grey and glistening wet. Nell stopped, hooked her feet round the bottom of the low metal gate. It swung open with a reluctant groan.

'Shortcut to Nan's,' she said. She jumped down, pointed. 'Bit of broken fence the other side.'

'Wait,' Billie said. 'When are you going? To Grassington?'

'Six or seven o'clock Saturday morning, or summat, I 'spect,' Nell said, standing still for once. 'In the dark. We get there early, park Florence in a field near the fair, like. So's we don't get stuck in traffic. *Life's too short to sit behind trucks and tractors, our Nell*, that's what me nan says.'

Nell looked up, held out her hand, as if she'd just noticed the sliding rain that had plastered her hair to her head and was dripping off her nose.

'It never rains for Grassington Fair,' she said, her face serious. 'But sometimes, it snows, just like someone ordered it, to make things extra-special Christmassy . . .'

Billie remembered, just for a moment, the small Billie that had wished for Christmas snow, exchanged cards thick with glittery glue with friends; listened for the jingle of bells in the night. She glimpsed her happy face as if through a frosted window: blurred and fuzzy at the edges. The other Billie disappeared, just like her Christmas glitter friends.

'Wanna come with us, do you?' Nell shouted, as she hop-skipped backwards towards the slide. 'I can ask Nan. She'll say yes. She will. Florence has got loads of room . . .'

Billie shook her head. She was grounded. No chance of Daniel letting her go on a trip like that. No chance of Mam persuading him.

'Can't,' she shouted. 'Thanks, though. Have a good time.' She waved, lowered her head against rods of rain that stung her face as she turned to hurry away.

But she *would* go with Nell and Nan to Grassington. She'd find a way. She'd hide, hitch a ride in Florence. Somehow.

Worry worms tangled with butterflies of excitement. She'd never seen inside Florence, had no idea how to get in unnoticed; or if there'd be anywhere to tuck herself out of sight if she managed it. The old campervan might be brightly painted and cheerful, but she was a rounded, dumpy shape. But perhaps she was bigger than she looked. Billie's heartbeat thumped in time with her quick feet on the wet pavement. What if Nell's nan saw her; told Mam. And Daniel . . .

It was a risk. But Billie couldn't miss this chance. It was perfect. As her footsteps echoed in the empty stairwell of the flats, a small space opened in the messy tangle in her stomach. A quiet space, where hope nestled. Nell, Florence, the trip to Grassington Fair – somehow, it was all meant to be. All part of a plan.

A plan that had started with a bedraggled black bird by a spindly tree.

Her beautiful, beautiful Bird.

TWENTY-TWO

The Friday evening sky – and Daniel's loud TV news – promised freezing fog for Saturday morning in the north-east; brighter weather to follow. The kind of crisp, cold brightness that might herald snow. Certainly a heavy frost by night. Billie prepared as best she could for everything, knowing that whatever she took would be no match for a winter night out in the open on the Dales. She needed to get to Dad before nightfall . . .

She barely slept. Her worry worms whirled and nipped. Hopeful butterflies flittered among them. She sweated under the layers of vest, T-shirts and fleece she'd dressed in, hoping to carry some stored warmth out into the early morning when the time came. She stared at the face of her alarm clock. The pointers ticked slowly on. Tendrils of the promised fog sneaked through her broken windowpane like icy breath held on the air. Daniel, free from Friday work commitments, crashed back from a *bit of extra downtime with the lads* and blundered around the hall and kitchen. Mam's voice filtered through his mumbles and curses. Billie smelled toast. Then the stumbling footsteps to the bathroom. Mam's anxious whispering. The creak-clunk of their bedroom door. Three a.m. on the clock face. They'd sleep late the next morning. Two more hours, and Billie would be gone. How many more before they noticed she was missing?

Daniel's snores filled the hallway, covered the groan of Billie's own door; the whisper of her mouse-steps to the bathroom and kitchen, backpack heavy on her shoulders, boots swinging from one hand. Minutes later, she was outside, her bag swollen with flask of hot chocolate, bread, cheese, apples – even mini packets of cereal and the family-size bag of peanuts that Daniel would normally finish by himself on a Sunday.

The fog had thickened. It draped itself around Billie like icy muslin, blurred her view and clogged her throat as she set off for Nell's house. She shivered inside her purple coat, pulled her hat down low over her ears. She had Dad's Arctic fleece and his waterproofs scrunched at the bottom of her bag, saved for the worst of any wild weather she might face in the Dales. No good wearing them now, or she wouldn't feel the benefit.

Florence's curved roof and bonnet loomed like small

purple whales in a foggy sea. Light from the street lamp opposite filtered through the fog in thin, pale fingers, picked out the silver trim of her round headlights in places. But her 'smile' was greyed out; invisible.

Nell's house was still in darkness, curtains closed against the winter morning. She and her nan were setting off at six or seven o'clock, so they'd be up and about soon, surely. But what if the fog didn't let up like the forecast said? Nell's nan couldn't drive in this. No one could. Would this be the first time she'd miss the Grassington Christmas Fair? Would it even go ahead?

Billie looked up. There was no way to read the sky story at this early hour. She'd just have to wait. And hope. She stood on tiptoe and rubbed at the nearest of Florence's neat, curtained windows. She couldn't see a thing. She felt for a door handle, pressed it down. Locked. Of course it was. What now?

A light at an upstairs window. A curtain pulled aside. A small face, pale as the moon. Nell was up. Had she seen Billie?

Billie ducked, crept around the other side of Florence, and hurried down the short alley where she was parked. She made out a tall wooden gate, a circular handle. The gate opened on silent hinges. Billie stepped into a paved yard – a garden of sorts, pots with winter-thin plants and round bushes visible through the fog, their colour stolen as if in a photographic negative. A second light flicked on in the house: a small yellow oblong in a back room. At the same moment, the sky above the rooftop brightened, just a little – either the moon slipping low or the sun poking its head above the horizon. Billie needed to keep out of sight, wait for Nell and Nan to start packing up the van; wait for a chance to sneak inside, unnoticed. If that didn't work out, she'd have to try and catch Nell's attention, persuade her to help her hide inside Florence. But that was much more risky: even if Nell agreed, her face would tell a story louder than any words, and Nan, by the sound of her, would be able to read it. She couldn't know that Billie was there. And she couldn't know why. She might have a purple campervan, but she was still a grown-up. She'd never let Billie go with them. Even if Billie told her about Dad. About Daniel and the ice-splinter silences. She'd want to talk to Mam. Maybe even the police.

Billie squinted through the fog. Made out a dark, squarish shape ahead – a shed? Billie moved cat-careful, hands stretched out in front of her so she didn't stumble over some unseen obstacle and make her presence known.

The door opened. She slipped inside, felt the drape of

cobwebs on her cheek. There was the warm scent of pine, soil and something sickly sweet that suggested mice like they'd had in the loft at Lambert Drive. Something soft and springy nudged her leg: sacks of some sort – rough fabric, springy and spiky: perhaps straw inside them. She delved in her bag, risked a momentary flash from her torch. Garden tools lining the walls, bags of winter bird food; seed trays, empty now, stacked ready for spring perhaps. A pile of checked blankets that spoke of summer picnics or windy winter trips in Florence. Billie pulled one around herself, folded another on top of one of the sacks, and curled up to wait for the dawn light. Even with the door cracked open so that she could see the house, watch for downstairs lights – there was some respite from the icy-fingered fog.

TWENTY-THREE

It couldn't have been more than an hour before strobes of pale light filtered in through cracks in the wood panelling, stretched in long stripes from the doorway. To Billie, curled in the dusty, dank darkness, it felt like forever.

She straightened out her stiff limbs, edged her head and shoulders around the door. It was a different world already. The fog had partially lifted. It hovered in patchy land-clouds a metre above the garden, translucent, ghostly in the semi-darkness and streams of light from the downstairs windows. Dew – or frost – trembled on the small lawn and potted plants.

A door slammed. A metallic, car-door kind of slam. Voices: Nell's, pure and clear as early birdsong. Another, older; hushing her. *People are still in their beds, our Nell.*

Were they leaving? Without her? Billie's hammer-heart battered her ribs.

She crept across the garden, boots darkening as she stumbled from path to lawn in her haste.

No. Florence stood with her side doors flung wide, like a bright bird ready to take flight. Billie peeped inside. In the front, seats for driver and passenger, in the back, a tiny house, complete with patterned sofa, low table, a miniature kitchen with sink and hotplate – a bright green kettle taped to the top. Cupboards. A tall thin door that might be a cupboard – or a loo, if campervans had such things. Beside it, a heavy striped curtain, partly drawn on a circular rail. The foot of a narrow couch, or bed, was visible; on it a tumble of blankets and clothes.

Billie's heart sank. Florence was tinier than she'd imagined. Hard to see where she might hide. And Nell and her nan would be back any time now. Her thoughts spun in circles like the dust motes in the shed. Should she just go – make another plan? Did she have to come clean after all: tell Nell and her nan everything, beg them to take her to Dad? Could she risk that?

Come on, Billie. Decide . . .

A swoop of dark shadow. A clatter of claws on Florence's roof.

A low, throaty call.

She knew that sound. But it couldn't be . . . could it? An image of her ragdoll raven flashed though her head, still and silent on the garage floor. No. There was no way . . .

Was there?

Her heart banged against her ribs. She stepped back, stood on tiptoe, squinted in the half-light.

'Bird?' she whispered.

Then a fluster of feather and scratchy feet on her shoulder. The earth-and-air-scent of his feathers against her cheek. An explosion in Billie's heart. A great, dragging sob escaping. A too-loud whisper.

'It *is* you! You're alive!!'

Nell's voice, coming closer. Billie's drumbeat heart jumping into her ears.

Bird fluttered into the van. Billie followed, decision made.

'*Bird*,' she hissed. 'Quick. Hide.'

Bird glanced at her; spread his wings, fluttered up on to the stovetop, down on to the curtained couch. Disappeared.

Footsteps. A front door slam.

'Right, our Nell. Time for the off. Hop in, pet.'

Billie scrabbled after Bird, tugged the bed curtain closed. This would have to do. And actually, there was a bit more room than she'd thought. Bird stared at her, head on one side; nestled down in the tangle of clothing, eyes sleepy, unconcerned.

The sound of hopping, skipping, excited feet. 'OK, Nan.'

A small sigh. Billie heard a smile inside it.

A scuffle of shoes. A slamming of doors. One. Two. Headlights splitting the last of the foggy night.

A stutter-roar and rumble of the engine.

Billie's held breath rushed out. She stared at Bird. Panic shot through her: she hadn't slept. She was strung-out, lonely. Afraid. Was she imagining this, seeing things that weren't there? She reached for the round black head, felt the feathered softness of it under her fingers; the hard bones of his bird-skull. It was real. *Bird* was real.

He was *here*. And they were both safe. At least for now.

Billie flopped back. Bird wriggled closer. She stared at him, curled her arm around him, felt a settling in her heart. He'd survived. He looked fine. Billie had no idea how that was possible but there was some magic in it somewhere, she was sure. She and Bird were going to the Dales together. That, it seemed, was the plan all along.

And every spin and bump of Florence's tyres was taking them a little bit closer to wide, wild skies and to Dad.

TWENTY-FOUR

Billie lay still, moving only to stretch out her legs when pins and needles fizzed in her calves. She wished she could draw back the curtain, see the landscape changing, rushing by. She noted when Florence moved from the stop-start of town traffic to the smooth swish of main roads from the town; felt the bump and wind of narrow country lanes. Heard the occasional brush of spiky hedge or splash and tumble of a waterfall through Florence's old, ill-fitting windows. The waking chorus of birdsong rose as the hum and blare of cars waned. Cold air leaked in too: urban petrol fumes and factory smoke giving way to something cleaner, fresher; scented with snatches of vegetation or farm manure. She imagined the skies widening above her. Bird sensed it too; eyes bright, feathers taut. He made small hops and jumps. Every now and again, he added his throaty *cronk* to the morning birdsong outside. Billie tensed each time, but Florence continued on. Billie told herself not to worry. If Nell or her nan heard him at all, above the chorus and the rumble of Florence, they were hardly likely to imagine a bird had found its way inside the van.

A faint song drifted into the back: a thin, sweet wobble of a voice. A familiar tune. Nell, singing a Christmas song: the one about a star. The star. Over Bethlehem. Billie had always loved that one. It was Dad's favourite too. *A star messenger, Billie. Imagine, if you wanted to send a very special message, could you choose anything more special – more beautiful – than a single silver star?*

Dad. She was nearer to him than she had been for almost three whole years. She itched to look and see.

Florence was stop-starting again, her engine ticking and surging. Nell was singing 'Jingle Bells' now, interspersed with excited giggles. Billie slid from the bed, round the curtain and towards the nearest window. Surely Nell would cover any small sound she might make.

A street. Houses. Shops built from weathered stone – a loaf-shaped sign swinging above one of them: **SKIPTON BAKERY**. A market cross and stalls to one side, their canopies striped in red and green, boxes stacked beside them. Cars trying to squeeze through spaces built before cars existed, and some early shoppers, bundled in thick coats and hats.

Florence rounded a corner. Billie glimpsed the fat round towers and turrets of a castle high above the rooftops. Black dots hovered above them: birds – ravens, perhaps. Ravens liked to live in towers. Or was that just another story? She'd ask Dad . . .

The van swung to the right. Billie had to clutch at the sink so as not to land on the floor with a thump. She sat back down behind the curtain.

A winding road for a few minutes, then Florence slowed again. Stopped. The engine coughed and was silent. Had they arrived?

Billie dived for the cover of the curtained bed, pulled on her hat, slung her bag on to her back. Bird would just have to ride on her shoulder – or be tucked under her arm, if he'd let her – the bag was full to bursting. And she doubted he'd fit under her coat with her three layers for warmth underneath.

Billie listened. A voice, metallic and echoey in the distance. An announcement of some sort. Something to do with the fair, perhaps? A faint smell of smoke.

Next, the click-clunk of one of Florence's doors. A blast of air and the sound of Nell, whistling happily through the gap in her teeth.

The swish-rattle of the curtain . . .

Nell. Staring. Her mouth and her nut-brown eyes perfect 'O's. Her hand flew to her mouth.

Billie held a finger to her lips.

A slide of voice through the door. Nan.

'Won't be a mo, Nell. Just paying for the parking, pet. Quick as you can. There's one due in any minute . . .'

Billie widened her own eyes, silently pleading as best she could. Bird hopped forward, fixed Nell with his black bead stare.

Nell turned away, stuck her head out through the door. 'OK, Nan,' she called. 'Just comin'.' She swung the door shut, opened her mouth, closed it again. Billie had built a word roadblock for her too.

'Please, Nell. Sorry – don't say anything. Don't tell your nan. Just, I had to get here . . . It's an emergency. A secret one. I . . . I didn't know Bird was coming. He just . . . decided. I thought . . . I thought he was dead . . .'

Billie's own word boulders tumbled free, fell over one another in a torrent that took her by surprise, crashed into the silent space between her and Nell. The stolen letters. Daniel, his thunder voice, his ice-splinter silences. His stealing the air from all the rooms. Mam, being chipped away bit by bit without her noticing. His fingers that gripped and his fists that flew.

How he hurt Bird, left him for dead in the storm.

How she had to find Dad before she and Mam got swept away in storm Daniel too.

Nell's pink face paled. 'But them's bad secrets,' she said. 'Sad secrets. You're not s'posed to keep them kinds of secrets,' she said. 'Only happy ones. You have to tell a grown-up. That's what Nan says . . .'

A crunch of footsteps. Nan's voice.

'Ready, our Nell?'

'I *am* telling,' Billie whispered. 'I'm telling Dad, OK? He'll know what to do. He'll keep Mam safe. He'll keep me safe. *And* Bird. He'll know what to do about everything.' She gripped Nell's arm. 'You can't tell your nan. You can't. What if she insists on taking me back home? What if she rings the police and they go round to the flat and make Daniel angrier than ever because I've run away. Because I've told. He'll say I've told lies. He'll make them believe him. Then they'll go away and leave us on our own: me and Mam. And Daniel . . .'

Nell chewed her lip. Her face grew paler than ever. She darted to the window and waved at her nan, turned back. She gave her solemn Nell nod. 'OK,' she said. 'Suppose . . . long as you're getting your dad. This ain't Grassington yet though, Billie. This is Embsay Station. Steam trains, they got. We're going to watch for 'em, we are.' A flicker of the gappy smile. 'They're real old-fashioned ones. Like in *The Railway Children*. Look out the window. You'll see.'

Her hand on the door handle. The sound of Nan rummaging in the front seat.

'Wait, Nell: you won't say anything?'

Nell shook her head. 'Wait there,' she whispered. 'Till we get to Grassington. I'll let you out. Long as you promise . . .'

'Promise?'

Nell stood tall, pulled up the hood of her duffle coat and puffed out her chest.

'Long as you promise to tell. Even if you can't find your dad, like. You can tell me nan then. She's good at helpin'. Promise?'

'Promise,' Billie said, her fingers tightly crossed behind her back. 'I will.'

She *would* find Dad.

She knelt up at the window. Watched Nell and her nan walk arm in arm across the car park, Nell's pompom hat bobbing up and down as they went. Nan was tiny, like Florence; slight, like Nell – dwarfed by a long blue coat that reached almost to her ankles. Grey hair hung down from a red hat in one long plait and her boots –

Billie squinted. Her boots were purple.

They stopped at a white picket fence. Billie made out the dark stretch of railway tracks behind it. A footbridge from one side to the other. A cream and brown signal box with a scallop-edged roof sat on the other side of the tracks. Tall pines, rising deep green behind it, waved in the wind. A handful of people waited with Nell and her nan. A whistle sounded.

Billie opened Florence's window as far as it would go for a better view. A steam engine chuffed into the station like a colourful dragon: shiny green and black engine trimmed with golden-yellow bands. A few carriages: some red as pillar boxes, others brown and panelled like the animal trucks Billie remembered from a farm set she had when she was small. Plumes of white steam and grey smoke streamed from its funnels, stretched the length of the engine; floated away behind it in a long cloud. The train slowed, moved out of Billie's sight, presumably to stop at the platform she couldn't see. She heard it huff and puff and hiss for a few moments; another whistle. Voices calling.

Three people appeared on the footbridge. A woman in a scarlet beret, a teenage boy who scuttled down the steps, head bent over what was probably a phone; and a man lumping a bike bit by bit down the steps. There was a sudden hiss. Another grey-white cloud drifting in the air like a thinning veil. As it cleared, someone else materialised on the footbridge. A man, long legs striding; briefcase swinging.

Like in *The Railway Children*, Nell had said.

Billie's heart twisted. If only, she thought, she was Bobbie. If only that was her dad, walking towards her right now, out of the white cloud, sunset-red hair damp and curled by the steam.

The man – long legs, briefcase, hardly any hair – strode quickly away. Nell and her nan turned round.

Billie slipped down from the window. She called to Bird, who was admiring his reflection in the mini kitchen sink. He ignored her; began pecking at a silver chain that held the plug. Nan's key sounded in the door. Bird changed his mind, fluttered on to Billie's outstretched arm, let her carry him back behind the bed curtain, just as Florence's engine roared back into life.

'Next stop, Grassington,' Billie whispered. 'Almost there, Bird. Almost there. Just try to be good a little bit longer.'

Florence bumped over some rough ground and stopped. Nell appeared quick-snap, called Billie's name in her best – rather loud – whisper. She grabbed a spotted bag from one of the seats.

'Nan's flask of tea,' she said. 'And scones. She's wanting them now, before we set off. She's just nipped to the loo.' She peered out of the window, her small face scrunched with worry. 'So you'd better go.' Her eyebrows shot up, eyes brightening hopefully beneath them. ''Less you changed your mind? 'Cos she'll want to eat in here.'

Billie shook her head. 'I can't. Told you.' She shoved her arms through the straps of her backpack, stood up, stooped under its weight.

Nell's face fell. The eyebrows drew together in a worried line.

'You got food? You can take my scones if you want . . . I'm not hungry. Bird would like 'em, wouldn't you, Bird? They got cherries in 'em.'

Billie smiled. 'Thank you. But we're fine.'

Nell fished in a drawer, held out a ball of striped twine.

'Case you need it for Bird,' she said. 'Hawk people, they use 'em; tied to their wrists, like, so as the birds don't fly away. I seen it on the telly.'

Billie shook her head. 'No,' she said, patting her shoulder. 'Bird'll stay with me if he wants. As long as he wants. I won't tether him. He has to be free to choose.'

She titled her head to one side as Bird flew to her, folded his wings, and settled, feet heavy now on her collarbone through the padded coat. He seemed to be growing by the minute.

'He chose,' Nell said, with the trace of a smile.

'For now.' Billie fished in her pocket, held out a folded piece of paper. It trembled in her hand like the stolen blue letter-bird that had brought her here. She wasn't sure she should ask this of Nell. But the thought of Mam and Dad never knowing . . .

'Mam's mobile number,' she whispered. She pressed it into Nell's hand, folded her fingers around it. 'For your nan – just in case, though. Just in case . . .' Her voice trailed off; lost somewhere she didn't want to follow.

'What, though?' Nell said. 'Case of what?'

Billie pulled on her hat and gloves. She thought of the

snow stories in the sky; the icy winter whiteouts of Dad's Dales stories. The dangers hidden in the beauty of them.

'Just . . . in case – that's all.' She gave Nell the brightest, bravest smile she could find.

'Thank you,' she said. 'Thank you for helping us, "our Nell".' She poked her head out through the door; checked the coast was clear 'And thank you, Florence,' she whispered.

Billie stepped out into a winter-brown field ridged with mud. Parking spaces were marked with ropes, posts and bollards and flags. Signs in Christmas colours with pointing, painted fingers:

TOILETS.

STREET FAIR THIS WAY! WELCOME TO A DICKENSIAN CHRISTMAS!

She took a deep breath – her first thirsty gulp of Dales air. The air that Dad was breathing too. She made her first footprints in Dales earth as she hurried away, hoping that for once, she'd misread the weather story in the wide grey sky above the field.

Billie followed the signs for the high street and the fair, hoping that any of the other early visitors would assume a girl with a tame raven was part of the entertainment to come and leave her be. She heard a few gasps, a couple of surprised greetings, but she kept her head down and her hood up, pressing on as if she hadn't noticed.

The fair wasn't due to start until four o'clock, according to the signs, and Billie guessed it couldn't be later than eleven in the morning now. But the cobbled high street was already a hive of activity and colour. Canopied shop fronts were adorned with festive lights, and great swathes of them hung high above Billie's head, waiting to shine out as early winter darkness drew in. Braziers, already lit, glowed red with embers, baskets of fat, shiny chestnuts sat beside them. Stalls lined the pavements on both sides, some with tables resplendent in shimmering tinsel trim, others with holly entwined around their metal frames. White berries glistening in jugs of green mistletoe stood on another. Pink and white candy canes and old-fashioned glass tree ornaments hung from still more. Boxes and baskets stood piled high on tables. The shops were opening and serving customers. Billie glimpsed proprietors in long dresses and aprons, or caps and cravats, as she passed glowing windows or doorways. An enormous Christmas tree towered above it all, resplendent in red, white and green lights, enormous baubles, brightly painted wooden animals and mock candles in golden holders. A man in striped trousers, top hat and tailcoat was practising on impossibly long stilts, trying to negotiate the uneven street. He grinned at Billie and lifted his hat; jumped down, causing Bird to flutter in the air in a fluster of wing and claw. He took a steaming cardboard cup of coffee from an adjacent table and sat down. Bird eyed him suspiciously from the top of a street lamp, and only flew back down when Billie pretended to walk away without him. When she looked round, the stilt man was leaning against a wall, a silver phone clutched to his ear.

The air was crisp. It smelled wonderful: a pure, clear freshness mixed with citrusy spices and pine. But it was growing colder by the minute. The wind had dropped. Among all the bustle, there was a stillness to the air. The kind of stillness that came before snow . . .

The sky always told the truth, Billie knew. She mustn't waste time. Mustn't make a mistake with her route and get lost. Snow fell suddenly in the Dales. And so did darkness.

She stopped in a doorway, took her notes and directions from her pocket. Part of her wished she could wait, see more of the Dickensian Christmas that was forming around her – see the magic and atmosphere build as darkness fell and the lights shone out in all their glittering glory. But she needed to press on. She'd come back another time. With Dad. Maybe with Mam too . . .

Excitement surged like a warm river in her stomach at the thought of seeing Dad. She pictured his field-green eyes, the tears in them; felt the solid safety of his arms around her; the tipping of her world back to everything she knew.

Nerves stabbed under her ribs like sudden knives. What if he wasn't the same, though? What if Mam was right and prison had changed him? What if *they* weren't the same any more, weren't Dad and his Billie-Blue?

What if she didn't know what to say to him any more?

She shook herself like Bird in the rain. She wouldn't think like this. She couldn't.

She'd thought she'd lost Bird, believed that the worst had happened. And here he was with Dad's rainbows still dancing in his feathers, yellow eyes as bright as ever. She thought she'd noticed a slight new limp when he walked. But it didn't seem to bother him. Didn't slow him up. And he had come to find her, was still her friend. After everything. He was still *Bird*.

'It'll all be OK, Bird,' she said. 'I know it will. Let's go.'

Malham was too far to walk on a day like this. *A pretty route for hikers*, she'd read, *across higher pastures and moors, taking in the River Wharfe valley*. There was mention of a 'magical waterfall'. But it took about four hours. And that was in the summer. For adults who knew where they were going, were properly equipped and had no particular wish to hurry. None of that applied to Billie.

Normally, she'd need to take two buses from Skipton to Malham. They didn't run too often as a rule, either, according to her research. But she was in luck: special buses ran that weekend to transport visitors to and from the fair. There should be one any time from the National Park Centre if the town clock was right. She'd ask a stallholder where that was. The special bus would take her all the way; no need to change. So hopefully, she and Bird could make it to Dad's place before the snow arrived, creating snow-globe streets in Grassington and icy danger out on a darkening Malham Moor.

TWENTY-SIX

Billie put on Dad's waterproof jacket over her coat, tucked Bird underneath it. She had no idea how he'd behave on a bus for an hour, with several stops and starts, but if she could just get him past the driver and other passengers in her bag, she'd find out soon enough.

Bird did not want to stay in the bag. But Billie needn't have worried. She was the only taker for the Malham bus. Everyone else was coming the other way, *in*to Grassington for the festivities. The driver was distracted as she got on and dropped her fare into his hand, leaning out of the window, talking to another driver, arranging to meet later with their families, in time for a visit to *Santa's grotto with the kids* and mulled ale for the *long-suffering dads*.

The rhythm of the bus on the undulating route soothed Bird. He settled down to sleep, head under one wing, on Billie's lap; didn't even register two stop-and-waits along the route, or the old gentleman that shuffled into a seat behind them a few minutes in. Billie ate the sandwiches she'd made, drank a carton of juice. She rested her forehead against the window, mesmerised by the flow of stone cottages, grey-brown open moor, undulating hills that lay like purple, sleeping mammals on the horizon; low drystone walls; sheep standing together in groups, as if waiting for something only they knew was coming. The sky seemed to grow wider and heavier with snow as they drove. As they turned a sharp bend in a narrow road, Billie caught the glint of a low waterfall, tumbling out among rusty green ferns. She imagined it frozen as it flowed, a great sheet of bubbling water, stopped in time until the thaw came.

Bird stirred just as Billie spotted the signs for Malham village. Roofs came into view. A church spire. Billie wriggled in her seat. She should see it – any minute, she should see it . . .

And there it was. A huge, crescent-shaped limestone cliff, rearing above the village like a great white wave. That was it. *Malham Cove*, Billie thought. Much bigger, much more spectacular than the picture Google had shown her. *A limestone cliff, seventy metres high, formed in the last Ice Age*. Somewhere, there was a huge waterfall and gorge too, she remembered. *Forged when Ice Age meltwater created a cavern that collapsed . . .*

Dad would know it already, she was sure. But they would go there together now, investigate the wildlife and birds together. See the falcons pictured on the internet, but for real.

Maybe there'd be fossils too. Billie couldn't wait.

The bus rumbled into the stone-built village, alongside a stream that appeared to run right through the middle. *Traces of an original Iron Age settlement can still be found here*, Google had said. No wonder Dad had come to live here again. No wonder he got lost when he had to live in the town. So much history. So many different lives. Here, time stretched backwards and forwards and forever, like the sky. Billie felt her mind – her *self* – stretching too. Like she could be anything. Anyone. Like she could be herself. Fly free.

But only if she could find Dad. And save Mam from disappearing.

The bus pulled up outside an old inn built from grey-brown brick. A few brave, warmly wrapped customers sat at wooden tables, heads bent in conversation over food and drink. A blue-grey whippet appeared from underneath one of the tables, barked a greeting. Bird, unimpressed, ducked lower inside Billie's backpack and went unnoticed.

'Stay there, Bird,' Billie whispered. She eased the bag

over one shoulder. 'We have to ask for directions.' She looked through the open doorway of the inn. A warm yellow glow. Holly. Christmas music. As she stepped inside, the smell of woodsmoke. Like one of Dad's winter night fires in the grate at Lambert Drive. Or November evening air, scented with bonfires and fireworks. Billie's eyes watered, whether from the smoke, or the memory, she couldn't have said. Her worry worms distracted her, tumbling and twisting as she approached a young woman polishing glasses at a long wooden bar. Was Billie even allowed in here on her own? What if someone asked awkward questions about why a child her age was out in the Dales by herself?

What if she'd got the clues wrong, and she was *miles* away from Dad's place?

The woman was all smiles. But she didn't know Dad, nor a farm near Malham Cove that might have taken him on. But she was quite new around here. If Billie walked to Malham Cove – the big limestone cliff – about half an hour from here, she could climb the cliff steps up to the moorland. There was a farm there, she thought. And one or two cottages. Yes, that was her best bet. And the steps were the quickest way, she thought. But Billie should go now before the weather came in. Her face flickered with concern then. Billie had someone with her, didn't she? There was a grown-up around?

Billie nodded – not a lie, not really. Bird was with her. And Dad was around – closer than he'd been for years. The bar phone trilled, loud and out of place under the low ceiling and ancient wooden beams. Billie raised a hand in thanks and set off for Malham Cove.

She followed the winding limestone path the woman had mentioned, up through land that rose and fell in small, low mounds of flat winter grass interspersed with grey limestone islands. Snow already clung to distant hilltops so they looked like cakes topped with white frosting. It had moved in closer now. A few flakes floated past her as she walked, pure white stars that disappeared like burst bubbles as they landed on Bird's dark wings, Billie's coat, the stony ground. Bird fluffed out his feathers against the chill air. Billie's nose and fingers nipped.

The village stream ran beside her then veered away. The closer Billie came to the foot of the cliff, the smaller she felt. Her legs ached as the bottom of a roughly hewn staircase came into view. She sat for a while on a nearby gate, stared up at the sheer face of the cliff, searched for signs of nests. She thought of the sharp-toothed pterosaurs that might have circled there long ago, before the ice came and swept away their world. Bird struggled free of her bag, spread his wings wide and glided up, up, until he was just a black scar against the whiteness. Then he was gone.

Was he coming back?

Billie jumped down from the gate, stood at the foot of the grubby white staircase. She could see only part of it before it twisted and meandered up the rock face. The steps were rough and uneven, the surfaces worn away by feet and time. They glistened in places: partly melted overnight frost, perhaps. As the temperature dropped, they'd ice over again. How many of them were there? Even the bottom ones didn't look safe. But as far as Billie could work out, this was the way to Dad. Bird was up there already. There, circling again, surveying the route ahead of her like Noah's raven scout. He swooped closer, hovered on the air as if to encourage her to follow. She took a deep breath. It left her again, thick as a snow-cloud in front of her.

One step at a time, Billie, that's the way. That's the way with everything. Put your trust in Bird . . .

She counted as she climbed. Forty-three steps in, and the top of the cliff seemed as far away as ever, the steps more and more eaten away: some slip-slide-sloping under her boots, despite their thick, ridged soles. A wind arrived.

The air grew colder and colder, as if someone above her was blowing icy breath in her face, trying to drive her back down. At times, she had to find hand holds in the rock face to steady herself; had to take off her gloves to get a better grip. A sharp edge sliced the skin between her thumb and forefinger. Drops of blood fell berry red on the white rock. Pebbles of panic pressed in her throat. She wasn't getting anywhere. How many more steps were there? Should she go back? And if she did, what then?

But there was Bird. Always Bird. Swooping in and out, hovering low when she faltered. Plucking at her coat when she stopped, when she felt too tired to climb one more step.

And then, *real* snow. Big, dancing flakes, whirling through the air, stolen as they met the white face of the cliff. Ice on ice. The flakes thickened. Less space between them now. Quick-snap, they became a whirling, twirling, bewildering blizzard.

Billie looked up; looked back the way she had come. Scanned the thick air for Bird. Could see only whiteness. He was nowhere.

What should she do? She couldn't climb in this. She couldn't stay still, or she'd freeze, here on the cliff face, along with the creeping, crawling, soaring ancient ancestors. And Dad would never forgive himself. Dread gripped her, cold and hard, as if the ice was in her stomach, freezing her from the inside out. She felt impossibly small. She couldn't do this. She couldn't move. Suddenly, her legs gave out. She slid down one – two . . . three steps . . . stiff as a winter twig, on her stomach. Terror gripped her. She felt herself disappearing against the cliffside with the snowflakes.

Somewhere, a bird was calling. Raucous and loud. There was the beat and swoop of feather and wing. A beak plucking at her purple sleeve.

And Dad's voice, fighting through the blizzard.

Purple. Purple saxifrage. See, Billie. See?

Go on, Billie. Dad's waiting. Right at the top. Dad's waiting . . .

She blew on her fingers, put her glove back on and drew the hood of Dad's waterproof tightly around her chin. She shuffled and slithered, one step at a time. She blocked out the white terror of falling below her, peered through the tormenting whirl of the snow, followed the dart of black wing or the glint of yellow eyes. Twice, she lost her grip, bump-skidded several steps down, not knowing whether this time she would veer from the steps and fall like a loose boulder in an avalanche. Like the word boulders that had spilled from her throat in the back of the purple campervan, in front of the small, gap-toothed girl who had tried to help her. She slid again. Heaved herself back up.

Then suddenly, no more steps. She had done it. She had reached the top. She hauled herself on to flat, snow-starched grass. It was icy and knife-sharp against her fingers.

The whirling blizzard seemed less fierce there: but Billie was colder than she had ever been in her life. As if her bones might have turned to ice, would crack and splinter as she moved.

Bird was there, tugging at her coat, pecking at her snow-crusted hat with his beak. Hopping on and off her back. Pulling at her bootlace.

He was right. She needed to move.

'OK, Bird,' she said. Her lips split and stung as she moved them to speak.

Billie had no feeling in her legs, but somehow, they still worked. She stumbled forward, hands held in front of her, Bird now flitting on and off her shoulder. Movement brought flickers of warmth to her body, but her feet didn't seem to be there at all, even as they carried her onwards. Any time she stopped – even paused to take gulps of icy air – the yellow eyes arrived in front of her, the black wings beating the white air. Coaxing her. Believing in her.

Then, amber squares glowing ahead: not eyes, windows. The slope of roofs glimpsed through the swirling snow. Fence posts, rough under Billie's hand as she felt her way along them. The yawn of a gate. The lowing of cattle.

This was a farm.

Bird shot forward, dipping and diving. Billie struggled after him on her twig-stiff legs and frozen feet. A farm. Was this the farm the woman at the inn had mentioned? The farm with the cottages?

Had Billie found Dad?

A door yawned yellow light as she stared. Billie pushed towards it with every last shred of energy. Someone was silhouetted there now: man or woman, it was impossible to tell – shrugging themselves into a coat that flapped and tried to escape in the tugging wind.

A woman. It was a woman. Long hair whipping her cheeks. She stared at Billie as if she might be a ghost.

'Eee, lass,' she called. 'What the blazes are you doing out there? Here, get inside with you . . .'

Billie shook her head. 'My dad,' she shouted, spitting snow from her tongue. 'I just want my dad. I'm looking for my dad. He's got red hair and green eyes. He's tall. Does he work here?'

The woman peeled hair from her eyes and mouth.

'Aye, lass. I reckon he does. Well, he did. On and off, like. But he's not here now. Not this last week, neither . . .'

The woman kept talking, shouted over her shoulder to someone in the hallway. Her words split and splintered in Billie's ears.

Dad wasn't here.

She'd missed him. She was too late. It had all been for nothing.

The woman, the house, the snowy air whirled and spun, blurred together like water spreading across a painting. Billie felt herself sink to the ground. She closed her eyes; saw only a tiny, brave, purple flower, crushed and flattened against the snow. And soft, field-green eyes disappearing into a wide, wide sky.

TWENTY-SEVEN

A soft weight covering Billie. Snow. The thump, thump of her heart. Was she trapped?

No. Not snow. Something warm. Something . . . kind.

Light, gentle, orange. Dark shapes above her. A mumble of voices. Mam? Daniel?

Colours floating and swimming as Billie opened her eyes. Her arm, heavy-slow as she lifted it to rub them, tried to focus.

She was in a room. A room she didn't know. In a bed that wasn't hers: a wide bed, with cloud-soft pillows under her head. Wooden beams across a creamy-white ceiling. Her thoughts whirled.

The creak of a door. A small face: pale hair, solemn eyes. A gap-toothed smile spreading. Nell.

'Nan, she woke up! Nan, quick!'

'Nell. How come . . .?' Billie pushed herself up on one elbow. The room, spinning again, loose, kaleidoscope shapes and rainbow lights. She lay back down.

Two faces above the bed. One barely still for a second. Billie's vision settled. *Keep your head still, Billie, that's the thing.* Two sets of hazelnut eyes, one set round and bursting. The other, calm and crinkled at the corners. Nell. Nan. No doubt about that.

Billie's voice cracked like an icy puddle: she had no idea where she was, or how she'd got there, but she recognised the hole in her heart. 'My dad,' she said, struggling again to lift her head. 'I want my dad. I missed him. I've got to find him . . .'

Nan's hand rested on Billie's arm, gentle as a fledgling bird.

'All in good time, Billie, pet.' She held out a mug. Billie caught a drift of cocoa. 'Just drink this for me now. You got a bit too cold, lass, and you passed out; bumped your head a bit. Been to the hospital you have. Remember?' Billie didn't.

'Never you mind, pet. You: you'll mend. But you have to settle a bit; keep warm and still. No . . . No more adventures for a while.'

Nell jiggled her legs – as if fighting her feet to stay on the floor and not propel her into her usual hops and jumps. Words bounced out instead – her loud whisper a little less loud than usual, Billie noticed.

'The police came, and the ambulance, and they said you were lucky, but what were you doin' out there by yourself? An' would someone get that bloomin' bird out of the way while they saw to you.'

Billie smiled. Bird. Wonderful, brave, funny Bird.

Nell drew in a long breath, started again. 'You're allowed to stay at the inn 'cos you don't need the hospital long as Nan's watching you, and anyway your mam's comin' and Nan don't even mind that she missed half the fair for the first time ever in her whole life, and Bird's a hero-raven now –'

'Mam? Mam's coming?' Billie's panic pebbles tumbled back, stone cold now in her icy throat. She struggled to sit up. 'What have you done, Nell?' she said. 'I *told* you not to tell!' Her drumbeat heart in her ears. She needed to get up . . .

Daniel.

Billie felt Nan's hand in hers, dry as paper, yet warm, solid.

'Now you listen to me, Billie. Everyone is safe. No one needs to worry. Nell did tell me. And she was right to. Came looking for you straight away when I heard all that, and good job too. And it were our Nell that spotted your Bird. Back and forth, back and forth over Florence he were

239

flying, like a mad thing. Pecking at the windscreen when I pulled over. Nell said to follow him and that's what we did. Led us all the way to Coveside Farm, he did, clever little chap. 'Spect he reckoned you could use a friend or two, seein' as you couldn't say a word to anyone at the time.' She brushed Billie's hair from her forehead. Her eyes were serious. Nell's eyes. Eyes that knew things.

'Things with your mam, and this Daniel,' she went on. '*And* with your dad: all that's too big for young heads to sort. That's for adults to put right. I won't say more, but I know a bit about it, Billie. Once, a long time ago, that were me, trapped and lost with a Daniel, not seeing the wood for the trees; not noticing the brewing storm till it were raging.' She paused, held the mug to Billie's lips again, nodded for her to take a sip, smoothed the bed covers. She cleared her throat.

'Your mam's still stronger than you think, lass. Mam's instinct. Try to protect our chicks, we do, even if we can't protect ourselves. Soon as she noticed you were gone, she had the police round, got them out looking for you. That Daniel, he made himself scarce all right . . .'

Billie shook her head. 'He'll come back. He won't like it. He'll . . .'

Nan smiled. 'Aye, likely he will. And maybe he'll find

your mam waiting for him again, to tell the truth. These things can take some sorting out. But there's people: social workers, 'specially for families like you – don't worry your head about it now, but it's sorted. They'll want to talk to you soon. When you're stronger. They can see to it for your mam and you, to have somewhere safe – if she's ready for that. If not, then . . . well . . . they'll need to know you're safe from now on, pet.'

A heavy tear ran down the side of Billie's nose. Mam wouldn't be ready. What was going to happen now? She wasn't going into foster care, whatever anyone said.

She heaved herself up on to one elbow. 'I'm going to live with my dad,' she said. 'He'll say yes. He will. I just have to find him.'

'And find him you did, young lady. Though goodness knows how. Got yourself to the exact place he's been working till a week ago. No idea how you did it. You and that clever bird of yours. Must be exhausted, the pair of you. So, you leave things to the grown-ups now. Your job is to rest up here and get your strength back. And that's that.' She folded her arms and nodded, more Nell-like than ever.

Nell was in full bird-hopping mode now, eyes round as conkers. 'What about the other thing, Nan?' she whispered.

Nan held a finger to her lips. Behind it, she was smiling.

'All the better as a surprise,' Nan whispered. 'Come on, our Nell. Fresh air for you. Snowball fight, I think.'

'But what about my dad?' Billie said. 'Did anyone even get his proper address yet? Did that lady know where he's working now? Mam hid his letters and he didn't know. Or maybe Daniel stole them, I don't know, but the address was all smudged and . . .'

'All in hand, Billie,' Nan said, her voice firm, like she was underlining the words in the air. 'All in hand. Now sleep, lass. You need plenty of sleep.'

Nell turned and grinned as they left the room. Her face glowed like a Christmas tree candle. Billie had the feeling it had more to do with the secret surprise than the promise of playing in the snow.

TWENTY-EIGHT

She woke to the smell of hot buttered toast and the sound of hopping feet.

Nell, bright red cheeks, bright red sweater, was at the bedroom window, tugging at the heavy curtains and bobbing up and down like an excited robin.

'Nan says you can sit in a chair if you feel up to it,' she said, the words broken by breathy jumps. 'Come see the snow . . .'

Billie sat up. No spin of colours. Just a slight headache and a very empty stomach. She reached for her toast and took a bite. She wasn't sure she needed to see the snow: she'd seen quite enough of that for a while. But the sooner she was up and about the better. Nan had said it was 'all in hand' to find her dad, but Billie wanted to be sure, wanted to help at least. And Nell in full robin mode was hard to refuse.

The bed covers felt heavy as she pushed them back, her legs watery-weak beneath her when she stood up. The chair by the window was far enough for now. *One step at a time, Billie-Blue. One step at a time. That's the way . . .*

The snow *was* pretty. Large flakes, delicate as feathers this time, drifting slowly past the window and crystal white in the light from the inn. Since Billie had arrived the previous day, someone had draped a tall green fir with clusters of white lights. A single star at the top shot silver sparks among the snow. Nell was transfixed; silent, nose pressed hard against the glass.

'You got to keep watchin',' she mumbled.

Billie smiled. Shuffled her chair a little closer.

A truck pulled up on the street, its roof and tarpaulined rear covered in a blanket of snow. A farm truck, by the size of its wheels, Billie thought. Delivering vegetables or meat to the inn kitchen, she supposed. The cab door opened. A man climbed out. Wellington boots; yellow waterproof jacket and trousers. A woolly hat. He turned, and reached inside the cab for something, straightened up. Billie watched him through the dancing veil of snow. Couldn't look away. There was something about him . . . the way he moved.

The man stepped forward, looked straight up at Billie's window, swept his hat from his head and waved it in the air. Snow gathered in his hair.

His tangle of *sunset-red* hair.

Billie's heart soared.

She leaped to her feet, her watery legs now full of fire. She pressed both hands hard against the windowpane.

'Dad!' she shouted. 'Nell, it's him. It's my *dad*!'

She ran from the room and out into the freezing air. Her dressing gown flapped around her like wings and Bird sailed high above her head in the wide, wild Dales sky.

EPILOGUE

Billie and Dad lay on a blanket on the edge of Malham Tarn. Bird hopped between them, collecting crumbs left over from their picnic supper. Soon, he'd disappear to roost in the barn or the night-time trees, but he'd appear again, as if by magic, out of the early morning air, calling for his breakfast and for Billie.

This was their place now, Billie and Dad. *Until things got sorted*, anyway. Here, where Stone Age hunters once searched for food. Here, where animals bent to drink from the waters as they'd done for thousands of years. And here, Billie told her home stories, asked her questions, and Dad gave his answers.

He had never given up on his Billie-Blue. Thinking of her had helped him through every single day of his sentence. They were welded together like the grains of sand and ancient bones that had formed the rocks and great limestone tarn. He had come to their flat when his letters went unanswered. He had been turned away by

Daniel and a mam he didn't recognise. He had known something was wrong and he had gone to talk to people that could help. His new probation officer that wasn't Leon. A solicitor. That was where he was the day Billie came to the farm. Trying to make sure she was safe. Trying to do things properly and not make any more mistakes. So he could always be there for Billie. Always keep her safe.

There were lots of things to sort out still. It wasn't safe for Billie to go back to the flat, everyone agreed. Not yet. Maybe not ever. Mam was still trying to find herself again and no one knew whether she would open the door to Daniel if he came knocking. Not even Mam. It was complicated, like Nell's nan said. Like Mam said. Dad couldn't keep Mam safe. Only she could do that for herself. But she had special people to help her now. Billie hoped she'd make new friends too. Friends like Bird. Friends like Nell and Nan.

Mam had visited already, to check on Billie, to cry some of her tears, and to tell her she loved her. She might be coming again for Christmas Day.

For now, as it was nearly the end of term, Billie was allowed to stay with Dad – and then they'd see *how the land lay*. They'd have to decide about school . . .

Dad had a tiny stone-built cottage with his new RSPB

Centre job. There was room for two. Maybe even three, *because, well, you never knew what might happen.* One step at a time for now.

Dad felt at home here on the tarn, and so, already, did Billie. It teemed with the wildlife they both loved: water voles, deer, shy otters. In spring, Dad said, there'd be house martins, jackdaws, dippers. The peregrine falcons would nest in the great white cliff at Malham Cove. Bird – if he stayed – could find his own friends among the flocks of wild ravens; soar in the wide skies and take his pick of trees to raise a family in. Bit by bit, Billie would need to set him free to be himself.

Nell and Nan were visiting on New Year's Day. Nell was beside herself since hearing from Billie that it had once been a glacial lake – and best of all, had inspired Charles Kingsley to write *The Water Babies*. She couldn't wait to see it and she couldn't wait to see Billie and Bird.

She'd be in full robin mode, Billie thought, and she smiled a wide smile.

She snuggled closer to Dad for warmth, folded her hands behind her tangled red hair and rested back. The night stretched like a great silver-studded cloak above their heads. Billie dreamed of summer days watching the swoop of peregrine falcons over Malham Cove, of picnics on purple moorland, and endless adventures under endless Dales skies.

Readable, reliable skies, full of stories still to come.

Before long, it would be spring, and ravens would return to nest in Tanglewood. Billie would take Dad to visit them there.

HELP AND SUPPORT FOR CHILDREN AFFECTED BY ANY OF THE ISSUES FEATURED IN THIS BOOK

If you are worried or scared at home, perhaps because people are arguing, shouting or fighting; if you think you or someone else might get hurt, try to tell a trusted adult such as a teacher, a doctor or family friend.

But there are lots of other ways to find help safely. Women's Aid have created a special space to help children understand domestic abuse and how to take positive action if it's happening to you.

- **Hideout, Women's Aid:** http://thehideout.org.uk/ children/home/

On these 'Hideout' pages, you can read stories of real children like Billie, and how they found help. If you need help straightaway, there are telephone numbers for advice and for emergencies. And a way to hide that you were looking at these pages. There are even games and colouring pages.

Below are some other places you can visit for help or support:

- **Childline**: https://www.childline.org.uk/info-advice/home-families/family-relationships/running-away/
- **Young Minds**: https://www.youngminds.org.uk/young-person/
- **Children's Society**: https://www.childrenssociety.org.uk/information/young-people/advice/domestic-abuse